Tracks in the Sand

৩

BOOK 1

in The Ally O'Connor Adventures

Other books in the Ally O'Connor Adventures series:

Sarah's Secret   Book 2

Other books for youth by Mark Littleton:
Aliens Among Us
God Is!
The Book of the Bible
Light the Torch, Pass the Flame: Lessons from Our Fathers
What's in the Bible for . . . Teens
Kids' Book of Devotions
The Abominable Snowbeast, part of the Get a Clue Mysteries Puzzles series
Football, part of the Sports Heroes series
Summer Olympics, part of the Sports Heroes series
Soccer, part of the Sports Heroes series
Baseball, part of the Sports Heroes series
Baseball 2: The Lives of Christian Baseball Players, from Tim Salmon to Jody Reed
Mysterious Mansion
Phantom Custodian
Cool Characters with Sweaty Palms
The Secret of Moonlight Mountain, Book 1 in the Crista Chronicles series
Winter Thunder, Book 2 in the Crista Chronicles series
Robbers on Rock Road, Book 3 in the Crista Chronicles series
Escape of the Grizzly, Book 4 in the Crista Chronicles series
Danger on Midnight Trail, Book 5 in the Crista Chronicles series

Tracks in the Sand

Mark Littleton

Baker Books

A Division of Baker Book House Co
Grand Rapids, Michigan 49516

J
LIT

Published by Baker Books
a division of Baker Book House Company
P.O. Box 6287, Grand Rapids, MI 49516-6287

Printed in the United States of America

Library of Congress Cataloging-in-Publication Data

Littleton, Mark R., 1950–
      Tracks in the sand / Mark Littleton.
          p.   cm.   (Ally O'Connor adventures ; Book 1))
      Summary: When three families go on vacation to Corolla, North
   Carolina, fourteen-year-old Nick joins Ally and the other children
   as they attempt to stop a plot to harm the area's wild mustangs.
      ISBN 0-8010-4490-1
      [1. Adventure and adventurers—Fiction. 2. Mustang—Fiction.
   3. Horses—Fiction. 4. Endangered animals—Fiction. 5. Criminals—Fiction. 6. Christian life—Fiction. 7. Corolla (N.C.)—Fiction. 8. Outer Banks (N.C.)—Fiction] I. Title. II. Series.
   PZ7.L7364 Tp 2001
   [Fic]—dc21   2001037775

The information on page 126 is taken from *Outer Banks Magazine*, 1991–92
Annual, P.O. Box 1938, Manteo, NC 27954

For current information about all releases from Baker Book House, visit our
web site:
                    http://www.bakerbooks.com

To Nicole and Alisha Littleton,
my favorite daughters.
I hope you will read this
someday
(when you have time).

Contents

Cast of Characters

Ally O'Connor: A fun-spirited, fourteen-year-old eighth grader with a zest for life and a love for horses.

Mr. O'Connor: Ally's father, a tall, lean man with bright green eyes and a walruslike mustache.

Mrs. O'Connor: Ally's mom, who has the same blue eyes and auburn hair as her daughter.

Nick Parker: Ally's tall, strawberry blond, teasing friend, also fourteen and an eighth grader, who has an obvious crush on Ally.

Molly Parker: Nick's earnest little sister, an eleven-year-old blond with freckles and a pure heart.

Mr. and Mrs. Parker: The fun-spirited parents of Nick and Molly.

John Debarks: A smart, sarcastic twelve-year-old with light red hair who wants to be a Pulitzer Prize-winning photographer.

Kelly Debarks: A precocious ten-year-old with a mop of flaming red hair.

Mr. and Mrs. Debarks: Parents of John and Kelly.

Mr. Tomoro: A naturalized American citizen of Japanese descent who speaks with the accent of his parents; a widower and beloved neighborhood storyteller, who houses the largest shark tooth collection in the Outer Banks.

Dunk: Mr. Tomoro's playful and beloved black Labrador.

Mrs. Newton: Known to the children of Outer Banks as "Widder Newton" because her husband passed away long ago. She lives at the end of the row of beach houses at Outer Banks on Pine Woods Lane and keeps a great garden.

Pack: The short and squat follower of a criminal duo.

Lug: The tall, lanky, muscular leader of the criminal twosome.

One

Stumbling over Trouble

Ally O'Connor knelt in one of the valleys between the dunes of the Outer Banks. She studied the marks in the sand as June sunlight poured down, an avalanche of heat on her slender body. Mustang hoofprints etched the beach on these islands off the coast of North Carolina—but not one of the beautiful creatures was in sight. Ally breathed the hot air and sighed, wishing a breeze would kick up cool air off the ocean—for the horses' sake, if nothing else.

The Outer Banks offered mounds of dunes for miles, along with plenty of tourist shops, restaurants, and a wide shoreline with frisky waves to play in. Houses jutted up off the ground on stilts, crowded together in pockets and lazy-mazy streets, bending in all directions. Everywhere new houses were going up. Ally regretted the way the area had developed with building projects. The only place that hadn't been disturbed was the wild horse sanctuary.

The wild Mustangs had been brought to America, north on Chincoteague Island, by Spanish explorers in the 1600s.

Somehow the horses migrated south and ended up on the Outer Banks. Over the centuries, they had almost been wiped out by long winters with little food. Sixteen had survived and were now protected by law. Legally, no one could attack, corral, or even touch them.

Smaller than racing thoroughbreds or the Budweiser Clydesdales seen on TV, these horses were majestic. This Mustang herd, led by a gallant black stallion, was like those found on the Great Plains, sporting several colors, but mostly ebony black, rusty brown, and dappled white with gray. What mattered most to Ally was that these horses were wild. No one had ever ridden them. To her they were exotic and mysterious.

She had drawn pictures of the stallion several times from the magazine photos plastered all over her room at home. Now, as she bent over to touch the surface of the hoof-print-dappled beach, Ally heard footsteps crunching behind her. She glanced back and smiled.

"Hey. Goofing off, as usual?" Her friend Nick Parker waved. Nick was the oldest of the kids whose families vacationed together each year on the Outer Banks. He trudged toward Ally in his blue-and-white surf trunks.

"Any sign of them?" Nick shouted.

Ally peered at the hoofprints, wisps of auburn hair sticking to her sweaty face. "I think I've found tracks," she said. "They came out of the grass up there." Ally pointed to a spot about one hundred feet away.

The two fourteen-year-old kids had wandered far from the beach houses onto a lonely strip of sand that was part of the horse sanctuary. Nick stooped next to Ally. He was tall for his age, like her. "So they went surfing?" he suggested.

"Yeah, or maybe they've been playing beach Frisbee!"

Nick laughed at Ally's comeback and checked out the round pockmarks scarring the dunes. "I'd say they were hanging ten," he grinned.

"In your dreams."

Ally squinted down the beach, watching the heat billow off the sand in waves. She knew Nick had a crush on her, but she wasn't about to encourage it. *After all,* Ally thought, *I have goals. Like . . . like? Well, becoming a concert violinist. Drawing pictures of every animal I've ever seen. Becoming a world-class veterinarian. Things like that don't allow much time for boys, not even Nick.*

But if Nick could help me find the Mustangs, she mused, *maybe he wouldn't be such a distraction.*

Ally noticed the horse tracks were mixed up, shooting off in different directions. Some were small, others large and gashed deep into the sand. Some looked as though they'd been punched by a cookie cutter. Between the tangle of tracks were two lines of human footprints, one made by work boots, the other by running shoes.

Nick exhaled solemnly. "It's them," he said definitively. He closed his eyes like a magician reading minds. "This one is Snoop Horsey Horse. And this one is Poof Daddy. This one—let's see, I smell a waft of fragrance in the air. What is it? Ah, something new and dashing. Should I tell John Klein?"

Ally gave Nick a push. "You mean Calvin!"

Ally had always wanted to see the wild horses. "What about these human tracks?" she asked, worry in her voice.

"Maybe somebody's trying to capture them for the circus. The ringmaster will announce, 'And now our lovely Lady Ally and her seven hundred Spanish Mustangs. Come out and take a gallop, girls!'"

"You're cracked. Besides, there are only sixteen Mustangs left in the herd."

"Lady Ally and her sixteen . . ." Then Nick was suddenly serious. "Somebody's tracking them," he offered. "Work boots, right?"

Ally read a twinge of concern in Nick's gray eyes. The boy's sun-bleached strawberry hair looked salty in the searing light. He ran his hand through it, throwing the tousled strands back like a cool surf-jockey. "Let's see where they go."

The two friends plodded off. The horses apparently had meandered, several darting toward the crashing surf. Nick stopped and pointed. "Looks like one of them went swimming."

"Wouldn't it be awesome to see that?" Ally said, staring toward the frothy waters. "Like that scene in *Black Stallion* where the horse goes splashing through waves like he owns the ocean."

"You'll see it," Nick said confidently. "I ordered it up for the show tonight when I and my new love will be having a dinner of steak and Cheez Whiz. Want to come?"

"Get off it," Ally said, giving Nick an annoyed look. "Come on, I have a feeling we're going to see the horses any minute."

But something about the human tracks worried Ally. "Most people walking this beach were barefooted or wearing sandals," she wondered out loud. "Why would someone wear boots on such a hot day?"

"Oh, probably it's the people who take care of the area," Nick said. "Maybe a clean-up crew or something. Or maybe a chain gang!"

"A chain gang of two guys?"

"The jail down here only holds two," Nick countered.

"And where are the men with rifles guarding the chain gang?" Ally asked.

"Ah, that is the mystery!" Nick joked. "They float above the surface on anti-gravity boots."

Ally glanced at the trees above the beach. "Look," she said suddenly, "the tracks go off into the brush up there."

Ally followed them, running.

Nick caught up. "So when will you be my girlfriend, Ally?"

"When the stars fall from heaven."

14

"Aw, that's no fun."

"Best I can do. After all, we're only in eighth grade, Nick, and my dad won't let me go out with a boy until I'm in tenth."

"So you're saying . . . ?"

"Bug off!"

"Thanks a lot!"

The kids followed the tracks into the tinder-dry bushes. Small scrub pines, poplars, brambles, and lush dune grass were everywhere. Ally noticed a trail carved through the trees. Inside the overgrowth, dragonflies and horseflies buzzed about in crazy arcs. "Why did they go in there?" Ally asked, setting her hands on slender hips.

"Maybe it's a girl and a boy horse," Nick said. "Maybe he wants to kiss her, but they're hiding out here because, after all, they're only fourteen."

Ally rolled her eyes at Nick.

"Do you want to follow them in?" Nick asked, the enthusiasm suddenly drained from his voice.

"Yes, a little way, at least," Ally replied. "There're brambles all over the place in there. But let's just check it out."

Ally thought about the devotional time she'd had with her mom and dad the night before. They'd been talking about trusting God. *Was this a situation where she could trust him? Would he give her courage enough to plod ahead and be the first to spot them?*

"Oh, wow," she thought aloud.

"What?" Nick asked.

"Nothing," she said, snapping out of her daydream.

Nick and Ally crept into the woods, greenery growing above them like a tunnel. It was rough going. More than once, Ally stopped to pluck a thorn stabbing the sole of her foot. Around a turn in the trail, the two suddenly heard voices. Both crouched down.

It sounded like two men arguing. A single dune sloped between the men and the two kids.

15

Ally and Nick started up the dune in a crouch, stopping just below the crest. Poking their heads over the top, they saw a couple of rough-looking guys wearing dirty short-sleeve shirts and talking crude. The taller man had on a greasy red baseball cap. The other wore a bandanna over his stringy hair.

His back to the kids, the short man gestured toward a clearing. "They ain't here, Lug," he said.

"I tell you," the tall man replied, "we'll find 'em sooner or later. One shot is all we need, and they're gone."

Ally glanced at Nick, worry creasing her brow. "Do you think the horses are in danger?" she whispered.

The tall man turned around.

Both kids gasped.

He was holding a rifle.

Two

Something Isn't Right

"I think we'd better get out of here," Nick whispered. "These guys don't exactly look like lifeguards."

"Hey, you, stay where you are!" one of the men called.

Nick's heart began pounding. He grabbed for Ally's hand and missed, slid down the dune crab style, and hit bottom ready to run. When he turned around, Ally was still on the slope.

"We're just looking around!" she said bravely, standing up tall.

Nick knew he couldn't desert Ally.

"Hey," the tall man said, grinning through gapped teeth. He hadn't shaved, and his lean, withered face gave him a starved look. "Seen any rabbits?" He cradled the rifle like an old walking stick.

"Using a rifle so close to the beach?" Ally asked. Her hands were shaking.

"It's just a pellet gun," the tall man said. "We're huntin' rabbits."

Something wasn't right. Nick could feel it. The short man gazed at Ally with hard black eyes.

17

"Why did you follow the horses then?" Nick asked, scurrying back to the top of the dune.

The short man stared at Ally first, then Nick. His hair poked out from under the bandanna like dry corn silk.

"We're just playin'," the tall one said, looking at his friend. When their eyes met, he nodded, as if getting the story straight. "Hoping to see them, like everyone else roun' here." He grinned.

Nick pulled Ally away. "Well, we have to get back," he called over his shoulder. Once on the other side of the dune, he whispered, "I don't think these are the Bobbsey Twins."

"More like the Twins from Planet Trouble," Ally replied.

"Yeah," Nick agreed. At the trail, he and Ally turned, looked back, then disappeared into the undergrowth.

"I don't like this," Ally said, stepping onto the sand.

"For good reason," Nick replied, then asked, "Did you notice anything strange about that gun?"

Ally shook her head.

"That was no pellet gun," he said somberly, thinking about his dad's firearms and what he'd been taught about hunting. "It looked like a shotgun muzzle, or worse."

"Yeah, and I bet they weren't hunting rabbits," Ally added. Running alongside Nick, she shielded her eyes from the glare on the beach. She couldn't stop worrying about the horses. "I have a bad feeling about those guys," she said, "like when you're watching a horror movie and the music gets dramatic. You know, like something bad is about to happen."

"Da-dah, da-dah, da-dah . . ." Nick made the sound from the movie *Jaws*.

"Don't joke, Nick. This is serious."

"Okay, but what do we do?"

Ally thought again about trust. She'd learned to trust God in many situations, but wasn't sure how to do it in this one. Should she ask Nick to pray with her?

18

"Please, God," Ally murmured. "Get in charge of this situation."

"What?" Nick said.

"Just praying, Nick, that's all."

"You're always praying."

"It keeps my hair nice," Ally said a little sarcastically. *I can't trust Nick to understand,* she thought. But from the corner of her eye she saw Nick gaze at her, then shake his head. *Can I?* she wondered suddenly. "All right, I think this is serious," she said.

"And praying is what we should do about it?" Nick asked.

"You know what my mom says," Ally answered, stopping, a bit off-guard. "You can talk to God about any situation."

"Okay," Nick said, running on, "but I think we should pray and run at the same time."

"Good idea," Ally answered, catching up to him, and they sprinted off up the dunes.

"We Want to Go, Too"

When Ally and Nick came into sight of their summer home, their families were sitting on the beach under umbrellas. Like Nick and Ally, their parents had been friends since school days, along with another couple—the DeBarks, whose two kids were fighting at the moment. Ally, an only child, quickly grew tired of the constant feuding. But John and Kelly DeBarks were as competitive as two puppies fighting over a bone, bent on winning their father's attention by besting one another at everything.

"It's my turn now!" Kelly, ten, cried. "Daddy said!"

"You can't hog it all the time," John, twelve, retorted. His light red hair stuck out at odd angles.

"Oh, go point your camera at a dead crab, John," Ally shouted above their bickering. "You've been bragging that you're going to win the Pulitzer Prize with it."

"I am going to win the Pulitzer," John said, sidetracked. He let go of the video camera. It was the effect Ally intended.

"I'm going to win the Nobel Prize!" Kelly retorted, her flaming red mop glimmering in the sunlight. She walked off with the video camera and fiddled with the controls.

Nick and Ally plopped down on the blanket, out of breath and eager to tell their parents what they'd seen.

"How was the hunting?" Ally's mom asked. Her blue eyes sparkled like Ally's, and she had the same auburn hair.

"Well . . . ," Ally began.

Nick stood behind her. "We didn't see the horses," he said, "but we think they might be in trouble."

Both Ally's dad and mom listened as the story tumbled out. Behind them John, Kelly, and Nick's little sister, Molly, crowded around to hear.

"They said they were after rabbits?" John asked.

Ally knew John would ask two million questions anytime something ignited his curiosity.

"You'd better call the police," Mrs. O'Connor finally said, glancing at her husband, a tall, lean man with a walruslike mustache and bright green eyes.

"Go back to the house," Ally's dad told the kids. "Tell the police what you saw. It sounds a bit suspicious. Better safe than sorry."

"Do you think they want to hurt the horses?" Ally asked her mother.

"The police will figure it out. Tell them exactly where you were, though," Mrs. O'Connor said. "Who knows—maybe you scared off those two guys anyway." She smiled, thinking, *Ally has always had a great imagination.*

Nick jumped up first and started for the house. "You coming?" he asked Ally.

"Yeah. Wherever you go, I go."

"I don't need any Bible quotes right now," Nick replied.

"We should go back and get pictures as evidence," John added, impatience coloring his freckled face.

"Oh, no you don't," John's dad told him. "You're not traipsing back there while there are people walking around with guns."

22

"We haven't heard any shots," John said, pointing his camera at Ally and Nick, clicking it. "Maybe it was just a really big pellet gun."

"Not unless he's using mini-golf balls," Nick said.

"Whatever it was, those guys are up to no good," Ally said, standing up.

"We want to go with you," cried Molly and Kelly.

"All right," Nick agreed, "let's all go."

The five started off for the house nestled back from the beach.

"Why would those men shoot the horses?"eleven-year-old Molly asked, her sun-burned face looking like an angel's.

Ally didn't want her to be worried. "We don't know for certain that they were after the horses. It does seem kind of reckless, especially in broad daylight. But these two guys didn't look exactly like straight-A students."

"Not like me, huh?" John asked, only half-joking.

"Oh, they looked like you," Nick added.

"So you're saying they looked awesome?" John asked, striking a manly pose.

Ally laughed teasingly. "Yeah," she said, cocking an eyebrow. "Scary."

The kids mounted the steep stairway to the houses. Suddenly Ally heard something in the brush over the dunes. She waved her hand, signaling everyone to shush.

"What?" John asked, almost bumping into her back.

"Be still," Ally whispered.

"Ally's always hearing something," John complained, but Nick pushed him down.

All the kids froze. Something moved among the long dune grasses. The trees rustled in jerks and jumps. There was something big in there.

Ally groped forward on her hands and knees. Usually the horses traveled with the herd, but could this be one that strayed or was injured? Or could it be one those men were after? Was it stuck? Ally's heart pounded into her throat. She and Nick took a step. Then another.

The thing howled!

Nick looked like he was about to turn and run, but Ally grabbed his elbow.

A black Labrador dog exploded from the bushes, yowling and nipping at Nick's feet.

"It's just Mr. Tomoro's dog, Dunk," John said, snapping a picture.

Mr. Tomoro was a neighbor, an old Japanese man who owned a wondrous shark tooth collection. His dog scampered up to the kids and whimpered as if he belonged to them.

"Awww, the poor thing's got brambles caught in his coat," Ally said, bending down to pull a prickly thorn from the dog's foot. Dunk licked her hand as she gently drew the thorn out. Nick picked up a front leg and scrutinized it, then let go.

"He's okay," Nick pronounced, taking the dog's face in his hands and shaking him. "Little Dunk gettin' in big trouble? Is that it, Dunky Boy?"

The dog yowled with joy for the attention.

Ally pulled off other prickers. Dunk gave the kids one more friendly sniff and pranced off, his head high, tail lashing. "That Dunk really had me going," she said.

"Oh, you're just a dog-lover," Nick said.

"And a cat-lover, horse-lover, lamb-lover," added John.

"Crab-lover, fish-lover, bird-lover," sang Molly.

"Not a pig-lover, though," Nick said.

Ally gave him a wink. "Well, you're a good pig."

They started up the stairs toward the house.

Kelly announced, "I get to make the call!"

John contradicted his little sister. "Ally is the witness," he said. "She's making the call."

"I'm just going to dial the numbers," Kelly retorted.

"That takes real genius," John said sarcastically.

24

Ally glared at him, annoyed.

As they came within sight of the house, Nick said, "Hey, look, Dad's in the crow's nest!"

Ally looked up to see Nick's father, Chuck Parker, with a pair of binoculars in his hands. He had beat them back from the beach and waved at them to hurry.

"He wants us to see something," Nick said excitedly.

Nick watched his dad peer through the binoculars then call to them again. "I see one of the horses," he yelled, pointing. "Out past the edge of the sanctuary—on somebody's lawn."

Dashing all the faster, the kids' sandals struck the rough pavement in sharp slaps. They reached the house and hurried up the porch stairs.

Four

In the Crow's Nest

Most of the beach houses on the Outer Banks were built on stilts. The one that the O'Connors, Parkers, and DeBarkses rented had six bedrooms—one for each set of parents, one for Nick and John, one for Molly and Kelly, and a third one for Ally. The house included all the amenities—VCR, TV, stereo, dishwasher, everything anyone could want, on vacation or not. It even had a spa outside where people could soak in the hot tub after a long day sun-tanning on the beach.

The crow's nest was an actual sailor's lookout post made from a ship's mast. The owner of the house had settled the post through the middle of the house. You could climb up a ladder on it from inside and then out onto a little deck on the roof. If you went all the way from the deck at the roof to the top of the mast, you stood a good twenty feet higher on a little platform. From there you could see for miles, depending on the weather.

"I'm first!" Kelly shouted as the five kids clattered up the stairs to the top floor.

"I'll beat you," John called from behind but catching up.

Nick grabbed John's hand and whispered, "Let her go first."

"Awww," John slowed down.

Nick and Ally watched from the bottom as each child before them pushed through the wooden hatch on the roof.

Nick climbed quickly and stuck his head through the hatch, eager to scale the last twenty feet. Suddenly he looked down at Ally. "Hey, shouldn't we call the police?" he asked.

"Oh, I almost forgot!"

"We see one! We see one!" Kelly shouted from high above them.

"Come on up, Ally," Mr. Parker called. "Your dream is about to come true."

Nick held out a hand to pull her through the hatch, but Ally said, "What about the police?"

"Yeah, you'd better do that first," Nick said.

Ally started back down.

"Hurry then!" Nick said, hoping the horse would remain in time for her to get back up.

"I'll be right up," Ally said, backing down the ladder. "Tell the horse to stay put!"

Nick stared out over the houses. Sure enough, a small Mustang stood in the middle of a lawn, chomping on fresh grass. "Hurry!" he called down to Ally. The horse looked up. As Nick watched, a man ran out of the house, waving at the horse. It looked like the same man he and Ally had seen with the gun.

"Can I see those binoculars, Dad?" Nick said.

Sure enough, Nick thought, peering below. "That's one of the guys we saw," he told his dad, focusing on the yard. "It's the guy with the gun."

The horse ran off, and the suspicious-looking man followed. Nick surveyed the area, looking for the other guy.

28

"The police have to know about this," Mr. Parker told the kids.

A minute later, Ally poked her head through the hatch. "The police will be here soon," she said. "There's not supposed to be any hunting on this beach—or guns."

"Some man chased away the horse," Kelly informed her.

"It was one of the guys we saw," Nick said, handing the binoculars to Ally.

Everyone stood for a moment as Ally looked over. "It's gone?" she whispered.

"I'm sorry," Mr. Parker said. "That goofball down there chased it away."

"Then let's go try to find it in the brush out there," Ally answered.

"I think we might want to get a picture," John said.

Nick agreed. "I think the horses are in danger."

Mr. Parker surveyed the situation below. "Okay," he said, "just check it out from the end of the street, Nick. Molly, you and Kelly stay up here with me."

"But why?" Kelly wailed.

"Cool!" Molly said. "We can look out for the horses and the bad guys then signal Ally and Nick and John where they are."

Nick wanted to believe there was an easy and simple explanation for everything. But Ally's jaw was flexed as if she was ready for battle. They sprinted down the street, John in tow, with his fingers poised on the camera, ready to catch any action on film.

Five

Advice from Mr. Tomoro

Ally, Nick, and John reached the edge of the horse sanctuary. They stood at the end of the street and surveyed the choppy lawn. The grass had been plucked up in huge mouthfuls.

Ally laughed. "Look, you can order your own Spanish Mustang to mow your lawn."

The air had a crisp, salty scent. *And something else,* Ally thought. *But what?* A little trail angled into the trees and thick undergrowth. *The horses must have gone that way,* Ally thought. She followed the tracks for a few steps then stopped before a pile of horse droppings.

"Yuck!" Ally said, shaking her head.

John stepped back to focus his camera.

"You're going to photograph that?" Ally cried.

"Yeah, why not? It's evidence," John said, his face full of surprise.

She hurried ahead as John's camera clicked.

"Where on earth did that horse go?" John asked. He picked up a stone and threw it into the trees.

"Don't do that!" Ally cried. "If the horses are there, it might scare them."

31

Nick stopped walking. "I guess we lost them again," he said.

"But where could they have gone?" Ally murmured.

Discouraged, they finally turned and headed back home. From the street, Ally looked up at the crow's nest and signaled to Kelly and Molly. But just then a police car barreled down the driveway toward them.

"Here comes the rescue squad now," Ally said. Nick and John turned to face the cruiser.

"Are you here about the two mysterious men with the gun?" Ally asked.

"Yes," one officer said, then ventured, "Are you Ally O'Connor?"

"Yes, and these two are my friends. That's the house we're renting. We saw the man again just a few minutes ago—there, by the house at the end of the street."

The officer craned his neck around and nodded. "Okay, I'll check it out. You kids stay here."

"Thanks," Ally said.

"What now?" Nick asked, feeling frustrated because he wanted in on the action.

"I've got an idea," Ally said. "Come on." She started off down the main street.

"Oh, yeah, Mr. Tomoro!" Nick realized. He loved Mr. Tomoro's stories. The old man, a widower, took special pride in being a naturalized American citizen, even though he was one of the first Japanese-Americans to be put in a containment camp at the beginning of World War II. He liked having Nick and others come by to talk.

"If anyone knows anything, he does," Ally answered.

"Mr. Tomoro, Mr. Tomoro," Ally said in greeting when the three reached his house. John was ready to snap another photo.

"Oh, Ally-san. And Nick-san and John-san. Mushee-Mushee." Ally knew that was the Japanese way of saying hello.

32

"We were hoping to take pictures of the Spanish Mustangs," John shouted.

"Ah, very hard to do."

"Do you know where the last sighting was?" Nick asked him.

"I think they down this end," he said, speaking deliberately, as if measuring each word from his mouth. "Have not seen in while, of course. But they—you know—hanging out."

Nick laughed. "We know. We just saw one on someone's lawn."

"Yes. They very suspicious of people, though. Must be careful. They wild, not so friendly, though I gotten close."

Dunk sidled up and nuzzled Nick's hand with his face.

"Is the best time to find them in the morning?" Ally asked.

"Yes, they feed early then rest in heat of day."

"Thank you, Mr. Tomoro," the kids all said at once.

"Douitashimashite." That was Japanese for "you're welcome." Mr. Tomoro added, "Thank you for stopping by."

The kids answered in unison, "Do-itashi-mashe-te!"

Six

Making a Plan

Later that evening the kids played Boggle around the coffee table as their parents perused the local papers from comfortable chairs. Nick listened to them talk about the local news.

"Looks like a real local brawl," Nick's father said. "This big shot wants to develop more of the horse sanctuary. Too bad."

"A ruthless guy, according to the press," Ally's dad answered. "I wouldn't be surprised if he keeps pushing it until they cave in."

"They won't give in," John's father added, looking up from the evening paper. "Those horses are sacred around here."

"Nothing will come of it," Nick's father said with finality. "The only thing that would change the situation is if all the horses disappeared. It almost happened once upon a time."

Nick knew he referred to a number of years ago when the Mustang herd was down to less than ten.

Molly whispered to Nick, "Do you really think that bad guy you saw is out to hurt the horses, Nick?"

Shaking his head, Nick tried to reassure her. "No one would hurt the horses. They're a landmark!" But he wondered if Ally was right. Were the Mustangs in danger? Were those two dirty men employed by a ruthless land developer?

After their thirteenth game of Boggle, Nick took Ally into the kitchen and laid out a plan. "Let's get up early in the morning and see if we can find the horses."

"How early?" Ally asked.

"Before the sun comes up," Nick answered.

"Whew, you do pick the times."

"It's the only way," Nick said.

The other kids chimed in from behind the door, "If you guys are getting up to see the horses, we are, too."

"No way," Nick answered. "This is for me and Ally."

John glared at them, then smiled. "Then let me and Molly come. Kelly should stay back because she's the youngest."

"What are you saying?" Kelly said angrily.

"All right," Nick said, sensing defeat. "But I think John is right, Kelly. It's too early for you, and you're too young."

Kelly started to whine. "I never get to do anything. I'm almost as old as Molly."

"Shhh," Nick snapped.

"You'll be part of it when we find them," Ally said, softening the blow. "Let's ask my mom," she added toward Nick.

"But she might not let us go," Nick said, scowling.

"Well, I think they have to know," Ally said. "We can't just sneak out in the dark."

Mrs. O'Connor and the other parents talked it over until finally they agreed the older kids could leave the house by daylight, providing they head home straight away if they saw any sign of the two men. Though a couple of the fathers had reservations, they trusted their kids to not do anything stupid.

36

Nick winked at Ally.

She nodded back, then headed to the closet for some backpacks and to the kitchen for supplies.

As he lay in bed, though, Nick worried. *Could something go wrong the next day? Just how much danger were the Mustangs in?*

Seven

Destination: the Unknown

Kelly heard Ally's alarm ring in the next room at 5:20 A.M. When Kelly opened her eyes, Molly was already stretching. Molly jumped off the top bunk and was dressed in seconds.

"Be real quiet," Kelly heard Ally say through the doorway.

Kelly breathed normally and tried to sound asleep. *I'll show them,* she thought to herself. When Ally and Molly left the room, she set her alarm for half an hour later.

John and Nick were already in the hallway when the girls stepped into the cool of the lower part of the house. "Let's rock and roll," Nick whispered.

Their equipment had been piled neatly by the back door the night before. John had his camera, a pair of binoculars, and a flashlight. Nick carried a knapsack full of bologna sandwiches, orange juice coolers, and his Swiss Army knife.

Ally picked up the blanket they planned to lay on the sand where they'd wait and watch once they found tracks. Molly shouldered the other backpack full of horse goodies—ten carrots, twelve small apples, and a packet of that thick lush grass the horses liked—a surprise from Molly who had slipped outside after the parents' conference.

"Ready?" Nick asked, opening the door.

"Geared up," John answered, checking his camera for the twentieth time to make sure the film was ready.

Ally looked everyone over. "Okay, don't anyone scream if the going gets tough. That's when . . ."

"The tough get going," Molly and John singsonged, each knowing Ally's favorite quote.

They stepped into the gray morning, and Nick quietly shut the door behind them. The sea breezes kept things fresh, and it always struck Nick as odd the way the days could be so hot and the nights so cool. But he knew it was because of the way the hot air over the land interacted with the cool air above the sea.

After waiting for twenty minutes, the four tiptoed down the porch stairs as daylight broke. Careful to make no noise, they set off past Mr. Tomoro's house, third from the end, and then past the "Widder" Newton's, the last house on the street, where the horse had fed on grass.

Everyone knew about the "Widder." It was said she had a fortune stashed away under mattresses and behind paintings and furniture. No one knew, of course, whether she even possessed a penny. But Mrs. Newton did have a great garden, unusual for the Outer Banks where not much grew except sand grasses, heavy shrubs, and trees. She loved that garden and could be seen working in it at all hours. More than once she'd protectively screeched at the kids to keep away, and Mr. Tomoro had told the kids the wild horses had once dined on some of her vegetables and she had gone crazy, screaming at them and firing a double-barreled shotgun into the air.

Mr. O'Connor and Mrs. Parker had warned the kids not to get Mrs. Newton's dander up. *But there was no danger of that now,* Ally thought, as they hurried past her house. No lights were on. Still, the Newton property always looked eerie, as if it was haunted. It was one of the older houses in the area, tall—three stories—with gray paint peeling on the front.

"All we'd need is for her to rush out on her broom and sweep us away," Nick said.

The girls giggled, and John answered, "I'd like to get a good picture of her flying across the face of the moon, like the kids on bikes in *E.T.*"

"It'd probably win that Pulitzer you want so badly," Ally said.

Everyone chuckled again. They reached the slatted metal bars in the road that separated the fences. Horses couldn't cross, but cars and people could. The dunes and thick brush of the horse sanctuary lay beyond.

"If we can find one of their trails through the underbrush," Molly said, "we might find them in places where they've found 'succulent' grasses. That's what one magazine article said."

"So if we can locate one trail and wait by it," Nick added, "maybe they'll cruise by."

"It'll be icky going through that brush," Ally forewarned. "Bugs all over our shins."

"Should have brought a machete," Nick said, taking the lead. He didn't want to tell the others he was nervous about this adventure, something he'd never admit.

"Yeah, like your dad would let you," John said. "Machete Meister."

"Just a thought, Johnny," Nick answered, pulling rank.

"Ah, stop fighting, boys," Ally interrupted. "We're nonviolent folks, remember?"

Molly stopped and looked down at the soil. "Shouldn't we look for tracks?"

Nick knelt down beside her, took a fistful of sand in his right hand, and let it trickle out between his fingers. In the still veil of dawn, the place looked spooky. Nick whispered, "Let's keep moving."

Waves crashed, making a swoosh-gush sound as they rolled in and then back out. A slight breeze picked up, and Nick felt cold.

"Let's stay close to the dune fence," he said, turning on his flashlight and shining it along the path. "It'll be easier going, and there's only the beach grass. It's high, too, because of the dunes, and we might see something. Keep your ears open."

They filed along, listening to the sounds of the morning and the breakers shooshing the sea. Cicadas chirruped, and a steady buzz of crickets undercut the early-morning noises. The sun had sent out its first tendrils of pink and gold across the horizon.

Nick shone his flashlight among the trees every few yards. When he didn't see anything, he stood and swept on, taking long, bold strides as if he owned the island.

Then something rustled in the bushes ahead.

Nick stopped. "Hear that?" he whispered.

Everyone strained to hear.

"What is it?" Ally asked.

"I don't know. Listen hard."

Nick knelt, and everyone went down with him. Then they heard it again.

"O-whoo. O-whoo."

"An owl," John said. "Let's find him."

Nick grabbed John's arm as he started to walk in the direction of the sound. "We're here to find horses, not owls."

"But the owl might be able to give us some information."

"Like what?" Ally said, putting her hands on her hips.

"Owls are wise, you know," John wisecracked.

"All right," Nick said. "Enough! If we're going to find anything, it'll be in the first few hours. The horses siesta when it gets too hot."

"Okay," John said, still staring into the brush in search of his owl. "But don't say I didn't tell you."

Nick plodded on. They were far from the houses now, and he hoped for a glimpse of the Mustangs soon. Instead all he spotted ahead was a long bend of dunes, and before them loomed one especially high, at least ten feet above them. They had just begun to climb for a view when suddenly they heard a man's voice, muffled by the sound of the sea.

"We'll find them this morning, Lug," the voice growled.

"Hit the dirt," Nick whispered, and everyone lay against the back of the dune, barely daring to breathe.

"Who are they?" John whispered.

"Is it them?" Ally asked in a voice tinged with fright as much as curiosity.

"It sounds like the guys we saw yesterday," Nick mused. He raised up to get the first look, with the others close behind, creeping up the edge of the dune.

Eight

Waiting for Action

Kelly's alarm rang, and she rubbed her eyes confusedly. Rays of sunlight broke through the windows to fall in red-tinged slats on the floor. *The crow's nest!* she thought. *The other kids may think I'm too little to go with them, but I can see everything from up there.* Quickly but quietly, she changed from pajamas to blue jeans, a red blouse, and a sweatshirt. Climbing the stairs, she listened for her dad's snoring. Yes, there it was. She could also hear the crash of surf in the distance—two sounds she liked to listen to at night because they gave her a safe feeling.

When Kelly reached the main floor, she stood at the ladder on the mast pole, but before climbing up she remembered all the things she wanted to take with her. She crept into the kitchen, made a peanut butter and jelly sandwich, found the video camera on the apron of the fireplace, and draped her dad's binoculars around her neck. Back at the mast pole, she started the climb.

Kelly saw the glass hatch under the roof that was sealed to keep out the rain. It had a screw-in type seal with a

45

large circular handle, just like on a submarine. Nick's dad had taught all the kids how to open it. She took one last look around the rustic family room before shimmying through.

The wind had whipped up ocean waves, and Kelly could see them from the roof. She looked off down the street where her brother, Ally, and the Parker kids had gone. Listening, she heard only the sounds of morning. Birds chattering here and there were getting the early worm.

Kelly stepped onto the first leg of the rigging that went up to the crow's nest where a red, blue, and green streamer whipped in the breeze, ragged and frayed. Suddenly she heard a noise—a shout. She pulled up the binoculars and twisted the eyepieces until the trees and dunes far down the island became clear. Spotting nothing unusual, she decided it would be better to get to the top before worrying about some noise she couldn't decipher.

The rigging rattled and shook in the wind as Kelly climbed. It was always scary taking those first few steps upward. In a moment she had her sailing feet under her and stood on the first level. Again she turned out to the horizon and peered through the binoculars while the wind whipped at her hair and rattled the mast. Pressing on, Kelly went through the little square hole in the bottom of the top platform of the crow's nest.

"If the others had any sense," she said aloud, "they'd have gotten a walkie-talkie and had me tell them where the horses were. Did they think of that? No!"

Kelly began surveying the horizon for signs of anything. Though she could see a long way off, there was no sign of the other four kids. *They must be hidden by the dunes or the woods,* she thought.

"I'll find them," she said to herself, taking the video camera out of her pack. She used the zoom lens to look closely. Distant dunes, houses, and even a car or two beamed into focus. Down the beach, in the trees, she saw the top of something white behind the trees.

"A big RV?" she wondered aloud. "No, maybe campers."

She swiveled about, cruising the area, then set the camera down.

"Well, horses," she said, "where are you?"

Nine

No Rabbit Hunt

Nick and Ally spotted the same men they'd seen the day before down the beach at the top of the dune. The tall one trudged along with the rifle on his shoulder.

"All we got to do is inject one of them, Pack," the guy said loudly. Nick remembered he was called Lug and appeared to be the leader.

"But we got to be real careful. They don't like people," the short man said. "Don't want to get kicked."

"I'm taking care of you, Packy," Lug said. He hefted the rifle and sighted along it. "All we have to do is to shoot it into a flank and run. Then we get the two grand, no questions asked."

"Why don't we just say we did it and forget all this stuff?"

"Not good for business. Might not get 'nother job. Anyway, she'd find out soon enough."

Both men followed the track into the brush.

"Now we know they mean the horses no good," Ally whispered.

"Maybe," John said. "Although I think those guys have hypodermic guns—and they don't use bullets. Animal keepers use hypodermics, like at the zoo or some of those wild animal parks. They inject the animals with some kind of serum, usually something to sedate them so they go to sleep. Then they tag the ears or feet. Forest rangers do it all the time with bears and birds."

Molly, Ally, and Nick stared at John. "But what could they be trying to put in the Mustangs?" Molly asked.

"That's what we have to find out," Nick said. "I don't think they have any other weapons. Did anyone see anything?"

Everyone shook their heads.

"I think we should get the police, now," Molly said. "And your mom said we had to leave if . . . "

"That's right," Ally answered, all serious. "I think we should go for help."

"I agree," Nick said cautiously, but stalling. "But we don't even know for sure if they're doing anything wrong."

"You heard them," Ally said. "You don't think they're doing something wrong?"

"Well, I guess I hope they're just shooting rabbits," Nick said, a twinkle in his eye. "Let's just watch. We can't panic. It'll take a good half hour to get back to the house from where we are, and who knows where they'll be then? Anyway, the horses aren't here."

"Nick's right," John said. "We may be able to divert those guys and scare any horses away before they get off a shot."

The girls agreed reluctantly.

"All right, then," Nick said, taking charge. "Let's tail them till we're sure of what they're doing. Then we go for home and the police."

"I have my Nikkormat," John said, patting the camera hanging from his neck. "Knowing we had pictures would scare them."

Nick nodded. "Right. That may be the best weapon of all. Let's follow at a distance. But no one gets close. We don't know what these guys are up to and what they might do if they catch us."

50

"Hey, you know what?" John said, lost in thought.

Everyone turned to look at him.

"That developer Dad was talking about last night, the guy who wanted to buy up the wild horse sanctuary—I bet he's trying to get rid of the horses."

"You know, that could be right," Ally said. "My dad said he was nasty and ruthless."

"If they hurt those horses, I'll bite them bad," Molly said vehemently. Everyone knew what a bite from Molly meant, though only John had suffered it when he was taunting her about her freckles.

"Let's not jump to conclusions," Nick said. "They might not even be talking about the horses. There are deer around here, probably fox, and of course, rabbits."

"You know they're talking about the horses—the wild horses," Ally said soberly.

Nick agreed, "We suspect that, sure, but let's be careful." He peered over the edge of the dune.

"Hey, shouldn't we pray first?" Ally asked.

"Ally," Nick said, "come on."

"I think we should just pray, that's all."

"Why?"

"All we'd be doing is making sure God is involved," John said, then he looked Nick in the eyes and said, "Doubter."

"Hey, I'm not a doubter," Nick said. "I just think we should do something, not just sit around and pray."

"We're gonna do something," Ally insisted. "Let's just ask God to help us."

"Okay," Nick said. "Then let's get moving!"

Ally and John bowed their heads and in silence offered fervent pleas to God.

Afterward, the kids made their way around the dune, and before long, they found boot tracks mixed with markings left by the horses. About thirty feet away they found horse droppings, too, and a couple pairs of tracks heading toward the ocean. The sun's light had now split the sky open like a cantaloupe. It was orange with great swathes of light like streamers in a circle at the edge of the shore. In less than ten minutes the sun would be hot on their faces.

John walked beside Nick, peering through the camera. Ally and Molly followed them, keeping close. Voices broke the quiet again, muffled by the shrubbery. A trail marked the way.

Then a shrill sound: Nee-heee-heee-heee. Over and over again.

"The horses!" Nick whispered.

The foursome hurried through the brush and hid behind some trees so they could peer into the clearing, where several of the Mustangs stood in a ring.

"They're here," Molly said with amazement.

"I'm getting my camera ready," John answered, twiddling the focus and light dials.

"That black one is the stallion," Nick pointed out. "He'll be the one to try to protect the others if they're in danger."

Suddenly the two men with the hypodermic guns stepped into the clearing far down on their left. The man named Lug aimed his rifle.

"Now we know they're definitely after the horses," Ally said. "We've got to do something. And fast!"

"Are you gonna pray again?" Nick asked with a grin.

Ally nudged him, exasperated. "I can trust God walking, running, sitting, kneeling . . . even stumbling!"

"Yeah," Molly said. "That's what I say."

"Well, okay. I just hope it works," Nick said. He sounded incredulous, but he was smiling at Ally.

Ten

Caught in the Act

The black stallion called everyone to attention. He was whinnying angrily and had reared up on his hind legs, churning his front legs as if in warning.

"Wow!" John said. "I've got to get a picture of that."

From behind the trees, Nick, Ally, John, and Molly each thought how powerful the stallion looked—not to be teased. Ally kept reminding herself that these horses were wild, nothing like the tame beasts she rode bareback at home. Just then she saw the two thugs getting their guns ready. "The men—they're going to shoot!" Ally seethed. "What do we do?"

John held up his camera. The big black stallion reared again, kicked his front hooves in the air, then swung around. The other horses shifted behind. They were clearly frightened.

The kids heard Lug say, "We gotta get in closer."

"That stallion ain't gonna let you get close, Lug."

"We have to do it in one shot," Lug said. "And the stallion is the one to do it on."

"What'd you say it was?" Pack asked while Lug focused his rifle.

"Some contagious killer disease," Lug said. "It'll infect him with a new strain of a horse disease; then he won't be around long. Neither will the others, 'cause they'll catch it from him."

"And that'll be the end of the horses. Poof! Pow!" Pack said, sounding like a Saturday morning cartoon soundtrack.

Lug laughed wickedly.

Behind the trees, Ally and Molly gasped.

Nick grabbed Ally's arm and whispered, "Be quiet." After a few seconds he added, "It's a good thing we came. If we waited for the police, it'd be too late."

Through the grass, he watched the the two men take aim. The horses were closed off and trapped in the clearing. The only way out for them was back toward the men, and that was exactly what the thugs wanted.

"We've got to stop them," Nick said, ready to act. "Ally, you and Molly try to stampede the horses from one side. I'll take the other."

John promised to get pictures, some Pulitzer shots.

Ally and Molly slid down the backside of the dune and hurried toward the trees. It would be dangerous; the horses were not known to be gentle to people. But anger churned through Ally's gut, overriding her fear. To see the horses steamroll those malicious men into the sand would be only right as far as she was concerned. She hurried up the beach with determination. Molly followed, her backpack flying.

Nick took off in the opposite direction. He would stand up and yell, hoping to create some pandemonium that might confuse the two thugs. Then the four of them could take off running down the beach. Sprinting about fifty yards, Nick then cut into the trees. It was tough going. Brambles caught at his shins, scratching and cutting. He plunged along as stealthily as he could. Within minutes he found a tiny trail that appeared to lead back toward the open area and the horses. He followed it for a minute, listening intently for voices or whinnying. Soon he heard the horses trampling the grass and bolting back and forth about one hundred feet in front of the men. He ducked down and listened, creeping through the underbrush until he could see what was going on. The horses milled around at the end of the clearing, their eyes wide with fear.

Nick scoured the trees for Ally and Molly but saw no sign of them. A little closer, and then he'd be ready. He crouched down then slithered on his belly. The undergrowth was thick, full of crab grass that scratched and tugged at his skin. He worried about cutting his bare arms and legs then spotted an alley-like tunnel. With new energy, he crawled to it, inching closer to the clearing.

⁊

Back in the underbrush Molly whispered to Ally, "I can see the black stallion. Should I get out a carrot?"

"We don't want to feed them, Molly," Ally said. "We want to stampede them. We need to scare them away from those men and get some pictures to identify those men for the police."

Molly stared through the growth at the horses only forty feet away. She noticed the wind ruffling through the trees. The girls were downwind from the Mustangs. Ally sensed what Molly was thinking.

"There's no way the horses will catch our scent," she said. "They won't run until we jump into the clearing and scare them into action."

Suddenly Molly realized this wasn't a good plan. "What if they turn around and come at us?" she asked, her eyes widening in fear.

Ally chewed her lip thoughtfully. "You're right. Why didn't Nick think of that? Maybe we should stay in the bushes and just shake them around. We'd better not step out into the clearing where they can see us."

Molly nodded. Both girls worked back and forth in the trees, trying to get closer.

The horses bounded about in a little pack like waves, dodging one way and then another—in unison. The stallion trotted around them in a frenzy. He ducked his head up and down, snorting and rearing. He wove back and forth in front of the pack, never standing still, never giving Lug a clear shot.

The men crept closer from the far end of the clearing. Lug sprinted forward then stopped and aimed. Pack followed, gripping a tripod. It appeared Lug planned to fix the gun onto the tripod for a clearer shot. Molly stood with Ally near the edge of the clearing, protected by the bushes, watching. Suddenly Pack picked up a long pole and darted at the horses.

"He must be trying to guide them toward the rifleman," Molly thought aloud.

"We have to move quick," Ally said.

Lug took aim, though he was still at least sixty feet from the horses.

Suddenly one of the men turned around. Molly followed his gaze to a glint in the sunlight. *Was that John's camera peering just over the top of the dune?* She couldn't be sure. It kept bobbing up and down. "Maybe we should just jump up and shout," Ally said.

"I think we'd better do something," Molly answered. "And quick."

"Okay, on three. One . . ."

☙

Nick waited for the girls to appear at the other end. He saw John poke his head over the edge of the dune several times but not close enough to snap any pictures. John would have to stand on the top of the dune and probably even run forward a little. Nick knew that even with the zoom lens he might not get good face shots of the two men. He figured he would just have to divert the men, and when he started to stand, his knees were shaking.

❧

"Two . . ." Ally said crisply.

Crack!

At the same moment a branch broke under Nick's knee on the other side of the clearing.

Lug jumped from his position under the tripod. "What was that?"

Pack turned around and immediately spotted Nick.

Ally saw what had happened and didn't wait till three. She and Molly jumped up and started yelling. At the same time John started taking pictures. The horses whinnied. The stallion wheeled, darted forward, then stopped right in front of John.

Lug and Pack spun in confusion and then anger.

"Get the boy," Lug yelled to Pack.

The short man whipped around, and John got a full-face shot with his camera. He just kept shooting as Lug dropped the rifle and ran up the dune toward him.

Ally picked up a rock. She didn't want to hurt the horses but had to get them going. They pranced back and forth, unable to make the decision to run. She hoped the stallion would take her cue. She cocked her arm and threw, striking the stallion just enough in the flank to cause him to bolt forward. The other Mustangs followed, kicking sand in a frenzy at Lug and Pack, who fell to the ground.

❧

Back in the crow's nest, Kelly bit into her peanut butter and jelly sandwich and scanned the horizon for signs of the Mustangs or her friends. Just as she started to sit back, she saw someone standing on a dune. It was a guy, and he had something in his hands that he brought up to his face . . . *Was it . . . ?* she thought. Then, *Yes! A camera! It had to be John!*

"Hurrah," she shouted, then muttered, "All right. Look for the others."

Kelly peered steadily; the distance that separated them was too great. She couldn't hope for much, so she leaned down and pulled the video camera out of her backpack. As she scanned the area one more time, she saw the horses roiling back and forth in the clearing. Pointing the video camera in that direction, she focused, then pressed the button to get whatever she could on film.

Eleven

Molly Gets Away

Nick saw he would be caught by the men unless he could get into the clearing and sprint. He figured he could out-run the squat man, Pack. He dashed around the edge of the clearing toward Ally and Molly with Pack less than twenty feet behind him. It was a good thirty yards to the trees where the girls were crouching among the brambles.

Nick kept his eyes on them, sure he would make it. But when he bolted around, Pack had begun gaining, despite his clumsiness. "Stop, kid," he shouted at Nick, "I've got you."

Nick didn't see the rock that just peeked up over the topsoil, barely visible. His toe caught it, and he tumbled headlong into a tree, banging his head. Molly screamed. Ally stood up and yelled.

Pack shouted, "Don't move!" He had a knife in his hand.

But the stallion was charging through the clearing, and Pack didn't see him coming. Whinnying with savage anger, the big black leaped forward, kicking. A hoof caught Pack in the chest, catapulting him into the brambles.

Nick watched in horror, wincing from his own cut, then wiped the blood at his forehead.

"Over here!" Ally called.

Pushing himself to his feet, Nick staggered toward Ally.

Pack cowered as the stallion reared over him. Then it wheeled, snorted, and led the throng of Mustangs into the center of the clearing and to safety, crashing down a trail and across the dunes.

"Run! Run!" Nick yelled as he started running.

Molly and Ally didn't wait. They both scurried through the underbrush to the last few trees, then turned around and waited.

Pack still lay in the bushes, unwilling to move. Had he seen the girls? No one knew. But they hurried through the woods back toward the beach.

"Did you see that stallion?" Ally cried.

"He was great, wasn't he?" Molly said, still awestruck.

"I guess he knows which ones are the bad guys," Nick answered with a grin. They all turned just in time to see the stallion disappear down a trail with the other horses.

Pack lay in the bushes, looking beaten.

John was still shooting with his camera as Lug screamed and cursed at him. John, sure he could outrun the lanky thug, clicked one last picture, then turned and skidded down the dune. But the big man leaped from the top of the dune, tackling John at the bottom.

The two wrestled and sprawled across the ground, John's camera tumbling into the sand. He tried to wriggle away, but Lug pinned him to the ground. John couldn't move. He squirmed beneath the big man and screamed for help.

Lug slapped him across the face. "Who are you, kid? Tell me!" He grabbed John's shirt collar and shook him. "Tell me who you are!"

"My name is John. Captain in the U.S. Army . . ." John said, thinking he could outsmart anyone, as usual, and trying to wisecrack his way through this. "Serial number: 123."

Lug cuffed him across the cheek. "Don't get wise with me, kid! Where do you live?" Lug shook John again, shouting, "Where do you live?"

John rolled over and tried to curl into a ball. Lug grabbed him by the collar and dragged him up the dune. John closed his eyes to keep out the sand. His camera lay in disarray at the base of the dune.

Reaching the top, Lug surveyed the field, holding tightly onto John. The horses stood on the trail, waiting again, but in the clear. The stallion seemed to have them under perfect control.

"Pack!" Lug yelled.

The squat little man stood up finally, shaking. Feebly, he ventured, "The horse kicked me."

"Get over here!" Lug screamed.

Pack hesitated then scrambled out, keeping to the edges. The horses disappeared into the brush.

Still unsteady, Pack came panting to the top of the dune. "That big brute knocked me in the chest."

"Shut up," Lug said. "Don't be stupid. We got problems."

Lug pulled John to his feet. He told Pack to get the camera. The short man retrieved it and tried to open it then gave up. "Never could figure out these things," he said to himself.

Lug grabbed the camera out of his hands and gave it to John. "Take out the film, kid."

"My name is John. I'm a five-star general. . . ."

Lug grabbed John by the ear. "Hold this," he said to Pack, giving him the camera. "I'm going to teach this kid some manners."

He pulled back a fist like he was going to slug John. Then he shouted toward the end of the dunes, "You better get up here, kid, or your friend is going to be hurt all over, and bad."

"Don't listen to him, Nick," John yelled.

"Don't try and be a hero, kid," Lug snarled. "It'll only buy you more trouble."

ॐ

Nick and the girls stopped along the beach side of the trees. Everyone ducked down and struggled through the underbrush to get a better look. Creeping on hands and knees around the edge of the last parcel of brush before the dunes, Nick saw the two thugs standing on top of the dune. John lay at the bottom, curled in a ball.

"Come out now, or this one's going to lose some major organs!" Lug yelled, but not so loud that anyone near the beach houses would hear.

"What are we going to do?" Molly whispered, her face a twist of terror as she crept up to Nick. Ally was right behind her.

"Just stay down," Nick said.

Lug's voice swept out over the dunes. "Get up here, kid, or this boy is going to suffer. Now!"

Standing up and peeking through the brush, Nick could see John better. Lug had grabbed him by the collar.

"We can't leave him there," Ally said.

Nick watched a moment, then turned to the girls. He took his Swiss Army knife from his pocket and hid it in his underwear. "I'm going to give myself up. Maybe I can help John escape. They're not gonna hurt us anyway— that would be too stupid."

"Hurt us?" Ally seethed. "What about what they're doing to John now?"

"They're not being that rough," Nick said, looking back, then turning to the girls, sighing. "Okay, maybe they're being a little rough."

"Look, Nick," Ally said. "These hoods aren't messing around. We've got to go for the police. Now."

Lug yelled one last time, and Nick peered into Ally's eyes. "I can't desert him now," he repeated.

"Okay," Ally said. "But we can't all go. That's suicide."

"We have to think clearly," Nick said. "I think they'll tie us up and get out of here as fast as they can. They know we're only tourists. We won't be staying around for any investigation, so they'll just hightail it. If I can delay them, maybe the police will come in time to get them."

Ally looked at Molly and said, "I'll watch and see what they do with the boys. Molly, you go back to the house, tell our parents, and call the police. Just don't get into trouble yourself. Keep down and out of sight, and don't let them see you, no matter what. You may be our only hope of helping John and Nick—and the horses."

"Nick, what if they beat you up or something?" Molly asked, her eyes wide with fright.

"Look, I got us into this, and if I'm with John, we might be able to stall them until the police get here. Anybody got a better plan?" Nick looked from Ally to Molly and back.

"All right," Ally said. "I'm going to do what I can to get you both out. But Molly, you've got to move fast. We can't wait long."

Molly nodded. "I can do it."

She pulled her pack onto her back and started toward the beach. "Don't get hurt," she called over her shoulder.

"Wait," Nick said. Molly ran back, then he took her hand and Ally's. "Squeeze, and then let's go."

"Okay."

They all held hands a moment and squeezed. Ally said, "Dear God, give us courage. Let us let you work." Another squeeze by all, and the three let go of each others' hands. Molly turned and crouched in the bushes.

Lug's voice pulled Nick and Ally back to the crisis at hand. "I'm giving you to three, and then this John person here loses his front teeth."

"We have to move," Nick said urgently. "Hang tough, you guys." He patted Molly on the back. She crawled through the bushes until she reached the biggest trees.

Ally gave Nick a quick kiss on the cheek. Tears glimmered in her eyes. "I'll be watching," she said. "I'll do my best."

"One." Lug's voice was behind them. "Two."

Nick jumped up and ran down the beach toward the dune. When he saw that Molly was well on her way and out of sight and Ally was hidden in the trees, he shouted, "I'm here! I'm here!"

❧

Through her video camera, Kelly thought she saw John. She put on her binoculars then turned back to the horses. They kept milling around as if very frightened. *What is going on?* she wondered.

A moment later, the Mustangs ran into view again. She pulled up the camera and saw them charge out of the small space and head for the trees. Kelly followed them with the lens, tracing their tracks around in a wide arc. *Where is everyone?*

Then Kelly saw someone running up the side of a dune. *Nick, maybe?*

She shifted her attention and concentrated on the horses, keeping the video camera pointed at them as they dashed about in a wide semicircle. They seemed to know exactly where they were going. At one point they crossed a main trail.

It was fun filming the horses. Kelly was sure the others would be happy she had gotten it on her video. As she panned the landscape, she noticed the top of a white RV parked in the trees. She panned back and saw two people on top of a dune. *Could that be Nick and John?* Kelly couldn't make them out clearly and turned back to film the horses.

Tied and Gagged

Lug gripped Nick's arm and led him to where Pack and John stood. John was bleeding, his sweaty, blood-streaked hair in his eyes. The camera and backpack lay on the ground, broken. Nick told himself to stay calm and said nothing out loud.

"What we gonna do?" Pack said to Lug.

"The cops're going to get you!" John suddenly yelled with fierce determination.

Pack shook him and said, "Be quiet!"

Lug turned to Nick. "Are there any others?" He shook him by the collar. "You tell the truth, punk, or you're dead meat. Are there others?" He began to frisk him.

"No," Nick said coolly. "It's just me and John."

"I'm sure I heard some other voices," Pack said to Lug. "Didn't you?"

"I don't know." Lug grabbed the hypodermic gun. "You want to get shot with this or somethin'? You better be tellin' the truth or I'm going to bust you good."

Nick caught John's eyes. The younger boy was obviously wondering what happened to Ally and Molly. But

65

Nick just let his eyes flicker a second, trying to signal John not to antagonize the two thugs.

"Well, the horses are gone," Lug said. "Let's get back to the RV."

He pushed John and Nick ahead of him. Pack picked up the camera and backpack. "One of you tries to get away," Lug said, "and the one left is going to get it. You understand? So neither of you had better try anything. Got it?"

Nick said, "I'm not trying to get away."

"Yeah, well, see that you don't change your mind."

Lug had a two- or three-day growth of beard. His dark beady eyes blinked. With his thin neck and protruding Adam's apple, he looked like a turkey, but he was wiry in a muscular kind of way.

Pack was definitely the follower of the two, obeying all of Lug's orders and not seeming to have ideas of his own. Nick hoped it wouldn't be too hard to get away, but he couldn't be sure he'd get a chance that didn't endanger John. He could feel his Swiss Army knife sliding down his side.

The four walked along the dune till they reached a separation in the undergrowth, then headed through. Pack led. Lug carried the injection gun, following the rest of them.

A moment later, Nick spotted their dirty white RV on a flat spot among the trees. With the underbrush crowding in on all four sides, no one could see them from any of the sandy paths used as roads in this part of the Outer Banks.

Nick thought Ally could probably drive an RV. She had lived on a farm for years, so she knew how to drive tractors, cars, and trucks. She had once shown Nick how to drive a little motorcycle and a pickup. He fought the impulse to try and spot her, signal her, and devise a quick escape, but he wondered if she was following them.

Lug kept turning around and watching the brush, then quickly catching up, giving directions to Pack. "Don't think anyone's around. It's awful early. Maybe they're not lying. You're not lying, kid, right?" He lightly punched Nick in the back with the butt of the rifle.

"I told you," Nick said, momentarily winded by the hit.

"When we get to the RV," Lug said to Pack, "figure out how to get into this camera. I'll get these two situated in the back. You get rid of the film."

"What we gonna do with 'em, Lug?"

"I don't know."

"We can't stick around . . ."

"Just shut up, Pack. I'll take care of it."

Pack's dirty blond hair and almost invisible mustache made him look like his whole face hadn't seen a washing in months. His dark eyes kept flickering from John's to Nick's and then away.

What other crimes have these two guys been part of? Nick thought. He realized he should try to find out who hired the men to infect the horses with a killer disease. He'd have to listen to them talk when they thought no one was listening. He decided to just stay quiet.

Reaching the RV, Pack unlocked the door. Inside, beer cans were piled in various boxes on the floor. A small dirty kitchen was behind the driver's seat, but it could barely be seen under the piles of junk. The place smelled of the stinking, sweaty clothing that lay around over the built-in furniture and floor.

Lug led the boys to a room in the back. He opened a brown door to a room where an even stronger stench of mold and dirty socks greeted them. Nick grimaced, turning away as Lug let them through.

"Welcome to my boudoir," Lug said.

Nick saw one large unmade bed, unkempt, with dirty sheets. Two in-the-wall dressers lined either side. They were made out of wood, stained as if someone had chucked a pizza two years before and never wiped off the tomato sauce. The dresser drawers stood open with wrinkled clothing tumbling out of them. Several comic strips were taped to the dressers. On the walls were newspaper clippings about the horses that Lug and Pack had been following.

At the four corners of the bed were four steel poles from floor to ceiling. The poles were fixed to the floor by bolts.

Lug shoved both boys onto the bed. "Get on your faces," he said.

Neither of the kids moved.

"I said on your faces," Lug growled more fiercely, giving Nick a sharp punch in the back. He pulled a pair of long scissors off the shelf. "You guys don't cooperate, I'll start cutting your hair, then your fingers, then your ears and noses. Got it?"

He grabbed some duct tape off the floor and said, "Get on your faces, lying flat on the bed." Nick heard something clink, and he knew immediately Lug had picked up some handcuffs.

Lug turned and strode out the doorway for a moment.

While lying flat, Nick slid his right hand underneath his pants and moved the Swiss Army knife to the side. He'd need it—and soon. Next, Nick pulled it out and nestled it among the pile of sheets as Lug stepped back in.

"Put your hands behind your backs," Lug said gruffly.

John was already on his face. "You okay?" he whispered to Nick.

"Shut up!" Lug said as he took Nick's left hand and clicked on the handcuffs then closed the other side onto the steel pole by the bed. The handcuffs tightened on his wrist. Lug then cuffed Nick's right hand to John's left and finally fixed John's right hand to a steel pole on the other side of the bed. Lug then wrapped their feet and hands in the duct tape, first each boy's legs strapped together, then to each other. He wasn't worried about wasting tape, that was for sure.

68

Nick mouthed to John, "Don't say anything." But Lug was going to make sure of that. He wrapped tape over each boy's mouth. "This'll shut you two up," he said. When he finished, he tested each pair of handcuffs and the tape then grunted and left.

Immediately Nick and John began twisting and wiggling. Nick knew there was no way to get out without help. *But where was Ally?* He twisted around and jerked on the handcuffs to try and reach the knife. John murmured something behind the tape, but Nick shook his head, indicating they not try to speak.

Thirteen

Ally Stays Close

Sure to keep out of sight, Ally followed the boys at a distance. When she saw the two thugs push them into the RV, she hid in the bushes on the far side of the vehicle. She tried to make out what was going on inside, but the windows were filthy. On one side, someone had inscribed, "Wash me," and next to it, "I'm one dirty critter."

Ally would have laughed if she wasn't so scared.

She watched the RV for several minutes, thinking through several plans of action. As long as the two men remained inside, she couldn't do anything to rescue Nick and John. She certainly couldn't storm the vehicle like some commando.

She decided to watch and wait, and edged around the RV, creeping through the trees. It appeared that someone was sitting in the driver's seat of the RV, fumbling around, although the vehicle hadn't started or moved. She crept through more trees until she was behind the RV's rear large-frame window. *Is that Lug?* she wondered, peering in what she figured must be a bedroom. *Maybe this is where he's stowed Nick and John,* she thought.

On the other side of the window, Lug disappeared through a door, and Ally crept a little closer. She studied the vehicle again and caught the mirrors on the sides. "Can't let myself be seen in them," she murmured, moving directly behind the RV. Hidden by the trees, she determined how to walk up to the vehicle without being seen in the mirrors. Studying the window again, she couldn't see Lug or Pack.

Where are the boys? she wondered. Edging through the brush and taking a breath, she scrambled forward, waited, and listened. It sounded like Lug and Pack were arguing at the front of the RV. *If I'm going to help Nick and John, now's the time*, she thought. Holding her breath, Ally placed her right foot on the RV's rear bumper to look in the window. She was afraid of being seen but knew she had to take some risks. A ladder ran up the back of the RV to the roof. Grabbing a rung, she pulled herself up until she could just look inside the window.

Ally gasped. Nick and John were taped up and handcuffed on opposite sides of a bed. She could see they couldn't move.

Her heart booming into her head, she tapped on the dirty window. Immediately, both heads swung round. Her eyes met Nick's, then John's. She motioned a thumbs-up and mouthed, "I'm trying to help." But she could see they didn't understand.

She looked below her a moment. If she had something heavy, a bar or maybe a tire iron, she might be able to knock out one of the men when they stepped outside the vehicle—that is, if she hid and waited. But who knew when they would come out? And she wasn't strong enough to take on both of them, even with a tire iron.

Ally thought of writing something on the back window to tell the boys what she was doing and maybe get some information. She thought, *Do the two criminals have a gun? Or a knife? Anything lethal?* That was the most important thing. She began to spell G—U—N—? backwards, hoping the boys could read it.

Finally she tapped lightly on the window. "Do they have a gun?" she mouthed.

Nick shook his head.

What about the handcuffs? she wondered. *Where are the keys?* She started to write handcuff.

Suddenly the bedroom door started to open. Giving the glass a quick wipe, Ally erased her etchings and slid out of sight.

"Whoa!" she said, her heart drumming. "Almost nailed!"

❦

Molly had been running as fast as she could on the beach. Almost back to the houses, she didn't see a little pothole left by the waves and tripped, skidding into the surf.

"Ouch!" she cried and gripped her leg.

She rolled to her front and started to stand up.

"Youch!" she wailed again. "My ankle's sprained!" Moving out of the way of a wave, she gingerly set down her foot. It hurt—badly. *How could this happen now?* "Father God," she prayed, "please help us . . ."

Limping along, she thought it probably was best to reach the first house, knock on the door, and ask to use the phone. But there were several hundred yards of dunes before she reached it. Her eyes teared at the pain in her ankle and shin. Still, John and Nick and Ally might get seriously hurt if she didn't get help!

"Lord, I'm going to get there!" she cried into the wind.

Her eyes streaming with tears, Molly tried to run, but it was no good. She limped along, keeping to the lip of packed sand where the waves last touched so she had something solid under her feet. She gritted her teeth and kept going. "Lord," she murmured. "I'll just go. Just keep on to get there, whatever it takes!"

Fourteen

Stuck!

As the horses drifted out of sight on the other side of the road, Kelly could no longer see any of the kids on the dunes. She climbed down the mast ladder and rigging, then stole inside the house. It was past 7 A.M. Searching the horizon for signs of the other four had tired her. She picked up John's radio, went back to the roof, and turned it on.

Kelly listened for a few minutes, then climbed up the mast with the radio in her backpack. At the top, she scanned the horizon for signs of the horses and the friends but saw nothing. She let her gaze rest on the RV in the dunes. It had to be campers, she thought. They probably were asleep—and they didn't even know the horses had been right in their neighborhood!

When a news break came on the radio, Kelly barely listened until something suddenly interested her.

"Local police have cornered several gunmen holed up in Duck Liquor Store, which they tried to rob a short time ago," the announcer said. "The twenty-four-hour store had one person on duty who is now a hostage. Over a dozen officers and a S.W.A.T. team have surrounded the store. The gunmen aren't talking. We'll keep you updated as the situation develops."

Kelly picked up the binoculars and turned them south toward Duck, but the town was too far away for her to see anything. Then she picked up the video, focused the zoom lens, and looked for something to film. "I'm missing everything happening everywhere," she sighed.

❧

"Where do you guys live?" Lug yelled, ripping the tape off John's lips. It stung, but John only whimpered, forcing himself not to cry.

Nick tried to speak, but John interrupted, "Up the beach."

"So you're here on vacation?"

John looked at Nick, and the older boy nodded. "Yeah, we're here on vacation."

"Why were you looking for us?"

"We were hoping to take pictures of the horses. We weren't looking for you," John said contemptuously. "We thought everyone around here liked the horses."

"Not everyone," Lug said. Then he glared at John angrily. "You've really messed up things."

"What are you going to do with us?" John asked. His voice trembled a little. He didn't want to show Nick how afraid he was.

"We're going to shut you up."

"But we didn't see you do anything," John protested.

"Yeah, but you know."

"Why are you trying to hurt the horses?" John pressed, despite a frown from Nick.

"That's none of your business!" Lug growled. "Now shut up!"

"You're not working for the developer that wants to build on this horse sanctuary, are you?" John asked.

76

"Shut up, kid," Lug said as he stretched out the tape. "You tryin' to make me slip up? No, I ain't workin' for no development organization. People. I work for people. Just like everyone else. No one works for an organization. They all work for people, some of whom are nuts. Royally nuts. Like the birdbrain we got payin' us to do this job."

"Who's that?"

"Wouldn't you like to know." Lug started to wrap the tape back onto John's mouth.

But not before John managed to say, "The police will be here soon."

"Oh, they're not coming, kid! Don't you know there's been a big robbery in Duck? Some guys are holed up in a liquor store. All the cops are there! Nobody's gonna be around here for a long time."

John gulped. If that was true, they were in bigger trouble than he thought.

Lug laughed and gave him a sudden shot to the forehead with the palm of his hand. He finished drawing the tape over John's mouth. "I'm sicka listening to you."

⁊

The boys didn't know Ally was leaning against the rear of the RV, listening. She heard the big guy talking. It sounded like John was answering. She hoped no one noticed the streak left by her fingers on the back window where most of the word she'd written was rubbed out. She couldn't risk going on either side of the RV, though, because she knew she could be seen in one of the side mirrors.

Ally chewed her lip and wondered what she should do. *What if the men decide to pull away with Nick and John in the RV?* "Dear God," she whispered, "just give me an idea." She had to do something to keep them from pulling out into the road and going up the highway.

Stooping to peer under the RV, Ally studied the underside for something to break. She definitely didn't want to mess with the gas tank, but she traced the long drive shaft from the engine in the front to the differential between the rear wheels. She'd learned how to change oil by opening the square nut on the bottom of the oil pan, but she had no way of turning the nut. It might make a lot of noise anyway, she decided.

Then Ally's eyes caught the tires. *Of course! Why hadn't I thought of this before?* she thought. She took out her knife to slash the tires and make them go flat. That would buy some time for the police to arrive—and prevent the thugs from driving away. Ally knelt down and slid under the rear of the RV. Grease and dirty oil lay on the ground under the differential. Squirming to avoid it, she looked up and noticed several rust spots on the bottom of the RV. *The whole floor is about to rust out! Can I make a hole big enough to get inside?* She picked at the rusty spots with her knife, but the bottom was too hard to break. She crawled back from under the vehicle so when she slashed a tire she would be safe from possibly being crushed. Poising the tip of her knife blade against one of the tires, Ally gave a stout thrust. The blade just bounced off the side of the hard rubber. She stabbed again and again until she was panting, but nothing happened.

All those stories about people slashing tires must have been done with much sharper knives than mine—or maybe that was stuff that just happened in the movies, she thought. *Anything could happen in movies. But real life? That's a different story.*

Standing the knife blade against the wall of the tire and holding it in her left hand, Ally tried to pound the butt of the handle with her fist forcefully enough to at least make a puncture. "Come on," she said to herself, "there has to be a way." But—nothing. She only hurt her fingers. Sighing, she looked back and forth between the front and rear tires. If she couldn't puncture them, what else could she do?

With a gritty squeak, the RV's side door opened. It was Lug. Ally saw his feet step in front of the vehicle and turn toward the back. The big man's boots crunched on the pebbly sand.

Ally froze.

Fifteen

The Flat Tire Trick

There was no time to run back into the bushes. Ally knew Lug would see her for sure if she tried. She looked back under the RV, scrunched into a ball, and hid as close to the rear tire as possible. She labored to control her breathing. She knew she couldn't hold it long. Her heart was drumming as she gripped the knife in her right hand.

Lug was walking back by the side of the RV, stopping several times to look at something in the undergrowth. He scraped at something Ally didn't recognize, then continued whistling. *He's in a good mood,* Ally thought. *Too good for the kind of crimes he's committed.* She waited, curling tighter. *Please don't let him look under here,* she prayed silently.

Lug shuffled by on the other side of the RV, his boots kicking up little puffs of sand as he stepped. Suddenly he began talking to himself and swearing. He appeared frustrated about something. Ally thought that was probably a good sign.

"Old witch is nuts," Lug said to no one, harshly. "We're gonna land in the can for sure. No way we can get those horses. We're gonna have to give up on that, money or no money." He swore again.

Ally cringed and wondered, *Who is the "old witch" who was nuts? Was some woman paying these thugs for the crime?*

Lug's black work boots interrupted her thoughts, kicking up earth as they scuffled by the rear wheel opposite the one where she was lying. His feet moved back and forth as he opened a compartment in the rear. It sounded like he took out some sort of equipment and continued to talk to himself: "Why did I have to get into this? Pack is his usual idiot self. I swear, I'm outta here."

Ally remembered John saying the idea to hurt the horses could be related to the land developer. *But didn't my father refer to the ruthless person who ran the organization as a "him"?* she thought.

Lug grunted as he pulled something out of the RV's rear compartment.

Ally strained to see what it was, keeping her breath as quiet and even as she could. Lug's feet were less than six feet away.

Then something dropped onto the ground. Ally strained to see what it was. *A syringe!* Her heart beat wildly.

"This'll put out those two," Lug said as he bent down to pick it up. For a second, the lower part of his face came just below the bottom of the RV. Ally could see his lips twisted into a sneer. She lay still, hoping he wouldn't look her way.

Lug grunted again. "Gettin' old," he said, closing the rear compartment with a scrape. Dust sifted down off the sides of the vehicle. For a moment, he stopped, both boots pointed toward Ally.

Instantly, she knew what he was seeing. *The letters! He noticed the letters on the window!*

Lug's boots went up on tiptoes, and Ally almost stopped breathing. She pulled herself slightly around the tire to be ready for a fast getaway. But then he muttered, "Man, we gotta wash this thing."

As Lug made his way around the RV back to the door, Ally knew she had to move fast. *A syringe! Is he going to inject the boys with the horse disease serum? They could die!* Ally thought, afraid. Then she heard the voices above her. The two men were in the room with the boys again.

"Oh, please don't let them hurt them, Lord," she prayed.

But Ally had to act! Who knew how long the men would remain there or what they would do to Nick and John? Realizing there was no one to see her in the mirrors, she pulled herself out at the side of the tire and looked up, craning her neck around the edge. *There!* The air valve stuck out of the tire with a cap and screw knob on it. "Once they see they've got a flat, they'll have to do something!" she muttered through clenched teeth.

Ally recognized this was a special cap that allowed you to let out the air more quickly. You had to take off the cap then turn it around and use the "tap" part to unscrew the valve stem. She'd done it a hundred times on farm equipment. One time she'd scolded Nick for doing it to a friend's bicycle as a practical joke.

The tire was fixed right below the windows on the bedroom in the back. She slipped around and unscrewed the cap; it came off quickly. She turned it around and jammed it into the air hole where the valve stem was tight and slightly bent. She worked harder, giving it a twist with all her might.

But the cap broke!

"Oh, no!" she cried, then covered her mouth and listened. *Did they heard me? No. . . .* Voices above were shouting. It sounded like Pack and Lug were arguing. *Are they bickering over what to do with the boys?* Deciding they hadn't heard her and unable to hear them, Ally flicked out the Swiss Army knife's leather hole awl. She drove the blade into the valve and turned it, hoping to create enough pressure on the inside edge to turn the air opening. She heard a slight creak, like rust breaking. Then the tire valve stem turned. A second later a hissing sound broke the quiet. In another thirty seconds, the stem popped out onto the ground. Ally reached to grab it, then twisted around and glanced at the front mirror. No one was looking out at her. She picked up the valve stem and held it in place. The air hissed out, and she waited. Plans formed in her mind.

"Yes," she said under her breath, "that's the way to do it!" She looked up into the sky and gave God a thumbs-up.

While the air sputtered out of the tire, Ally crawled back to the end of the RV. Maybe she could do it to all four tires. Then she thought, *No, that way they'll know someone did it. This way, if I put back the valve stem, they won't know I'm here.*

Ally snaked back to the end of the RV and listened underneath the window to determine if Lug and Pack were still in the room. No sounds could be heard. She was tempted to take a look. Waiting and listening, she finally decided to give it a try. Climbing up the ladder, she looked in. Both boys lay on their faces, and Lug was bent over them.

She immediately ducked down, her heart beating wildly. She noticed the hissing sound was lower. The tire was almost flat. The RV had tilted slightly, but she hoped no one would notice until she carried out her plan. She listened one more time for voices.

Nothing.

Taking another long breath, Ally pulled herself up toward the window again, keeping to the side until she leaned to look in. Lug was gone. The boys were on their faces but wriggling.

Okay, she thought as she ducked back down and stood on the ground. *Get that stem back in, and then hopefully they'll try to move the vehicle or feel how it's leaning.* She crawled under the back end again and wriggled herself up to the tire. Glancing in the mirror, she saw no one was in the driver's seat. She replaced the stem in the now flat tire and screwed on the cap.

"Now just let them try to drive," Ally murmured. Luckily, Lug had not walked on that side of the RV, so he wouldn't have noticed that the tire was fine only moments ago.

Giving the mirror one last glance, Ally paused to see if anyone appeared. Suddenly Pack plopped into the front seat, looking grim. Ally immediately ducked back under the RV. She waited a moment then slid to the back of the RV, hauling herself up by the back bumper. She climbed the ladder one more time, peeked in, and tapped on the window. Both boys looked up immediately. She gave them a thumbs-up and smiled then jumped off the ladder onto the ground. Keeping the back of the RV directly behind her so she couldn't be seen in the mirrors, she stepped backward until she reached the woods.

Crouching in the brush and feeling confident, Ally said, "All right, you thugs! Just try to get away."

Sixteen

Boys in Danger

Nick made John understand about his hidden knife through murmurs and flicks of his head and eyes. John slid forward on the bed as far as he could, and they both reached for it. Both boys strained, rolled slightly, pushed. No go. Then Nick felt a little lump under his chin. The knife was there—just under the sheet. Both of them scrabbled for position. Nick couldn't pull his hand close enough, and John's was stretched to the limit.

Nick murmured through the tape, "It won't work." He jiggled his chin, nudging the sheets and lump, trying to move it out from underneath. The sheet moved off it slightly. The plastic red handle with the cross in the shield was exposed.

Nick jerked it again with his chin, shoving it to the right. If he could slide it into the middle, they might be able to reach it with their hands. Just a few more inches.

The knife was plainly visible now. Just another three inches, Nick thought. He flopped, trying to jiggle the knife farther to the side. He squirmed, pushing himself closer. By moving both his eyes, he made John understand what he was trying to do.

A sudden commotion at the bedroom door made John and Nick freeze. They didn't dare look at the knife.

The door opened.

"This stuff'll put you guys out," Lug said as he set the case down in a corner. Pack stood behind him. "By the time you're awake, we'll be long gone."

Nick could see John motioning with his eyes. Out of the corner he could see the little nub of red exposed. If they saw the knife, what would the men do? Certainly not worse than they'd already done. But what were they going to inject them with? Surely not the disease serum!

Nick thought of trying to nudge the sheet up over the knife, but he knew that might just call attention to it. They couldn't cover it anyway.

Lug moved about, fiddling with the things in the chest. Pack was watching him, making comments.

"You sure we should do it now? They'll be heavy to move."

"We can drop them off anywhere then, idiot. You'll see. It's the best way."

Lug squinted nastily at the boys. Nick wondered what could be done as Lug drew out a hypodermic needle and a vial of liquid. "See, we're pros at this kind of stuff. That's why we was hired. We know how to get the job done."

Glancing at John, Nick made no other movement. He hoped Lug wasn't planning to inject them now.

John suddenly rolled on the bed, groaning and writhing. The movement pushed the sheet up, almost covering the knife.

Lug's eyes nearly popped. He sprang over to John, dropping the needle. "What's a matter, boy?"

John just writhed.

Lug ripped off the tape that covered his mouth.

Nick winced with a recognition of the pain.

"I'm cramping up," John cried. "I'm diabetic, and I'm cramping up."

Nick knew John wasn't diabetic. But he also knew that a diabetic could have convulsions if he didn't have the right amount of insulin. It was a good trick.

Nick started yelling behind the tape. "He'll die! He'll die!"

John squirmed on the bed, being careful not to move the sheets any farther.

Pack and Lug swore, then Lug told his friend to take the tape off Nick's mouth.

Nick cried, "He needs his insulin, or he'll die."

Lug looked from John to the box of needles. "I may have some insulin in here."

Nick's eyes popped. What would happen if they really gave John insulin? Would he pass out? Could he die? Nick didn't know.

"He needs a special kind," Nick said right away. "It's a special dose. It has something else in it."

Lug stood. "You're lying, kid. There ain't no special doses."

Nick insisted, "You can't just give him anything!"

John slowed down and then stopped, blinking and lying still. "I just cramped up. My thighs and shins. I feel better. Can I just lay here for a minute?"

Lug turned to Pack. "Go start the truck. Let's get on the road. Don't worry about the knockout juice just now. Let's just get out of here. Got it?"

Pack nodded. "What about the horses?"

"We'll look for them as we drive."

Pack sauntered out of the bedroom and shut the door. Lug gazed thoughtfully at the two boys. "You think you're pretty smart cookies, huh? Well, I'm a lot smarter. Don't go trying to fake me out. I'm gonna give you the shot anyway. And sooner rather than later."

Underneath the bedroom, the RV engine trembled then roared. The whole vehicle shook. Nick thought miserably there was no way Ally could do anything now.

The big vehicle chugged forward then stopped. A moment later, Pack was at the door. "We gotta flat, Lug."

Giving the two boys a sharp look, Lug set his teeth. "Those were practically new tires."

Pack looked at him helplessly.

Lug pulled John up by the collar just inches from his face. "You guys got a friend out there or somethin'? You're not pullin' somethin', are you?"

"You think *we* did it?" Nick yelled.

Lug slapped Nick. "Listen, smart boy, anything happens while we're out there, I swear, we'll hurt you guys real good. And your friends, too! You better not ask for it. Understand?"

Nick could see the knife poking out from the sheets, but Lug had just thrust him over it.

"Come on, Pack. Let's get this thing fixed."

Seventeen

Molly's Rescue Mission Stalls

When the engine roared to life, Ally watched the vehicle jolt forward about ten feet then stop. She realized if the men came out, she'd need to be on the door side of the vehicle to get inside and free John and Nick. She ran through the brush, watching the door so that she could stop and be quiet once the men emerged.

"Please, let both of them come out, Lord," she murmured, keeping her eyes on the RV.

The front door opened, and Ally stopped, crouching in the sand. Pack was saying, "If anything *can* go wrong . . . What's that saying?"

"It will!" Lug answered.

"What?"

"If anything can go wrong, it will!"

"Crummy idea," Pack answered.

"You got that right," Lug said.

Ally followed the two men with her eyes as they walked around to the back then to the other side of the RV. She had to move fast. She skirted the trees on the sand until she was opposite the front door.

"Now for the hard part," she said as she crawled on her elbows and knees down a small trail in the growth.

"Hurry, Molly," she said as she crawled. "Get the police here fast." Peering beneath the RV, she saw the legs of the men by the tire. *The RV tires are big,* she reasoned, *and those lug nuts are tight. It will take them at least ten minutes to figure out how to change the tire. Time to get moving.*

❧

Molly stood on top of a dune, her leg throbbing with pain. She'd taken off her windbreaker and made a kind of tourniquet, wrapping her ankle and shin in the back, drawing the ends of the jacket tight in front of her leg through the loops, and tying it. More scared than ever, she was about to limp back toward the ocean. There, between her and the houses, were the horses—sixteen of them—standing in the grass and peering at her with curious eyes. They were probably wondering if she'd pull out a gun and shoot them like the two thugs had tried earlier. She'd seen how the stallion had reacted to Pack. How could she go around the horses to reach the beach houses, another one hundred yards beyond?

The carrots! Molly dropped her pack and opened it. There were ten carrots, cubes of sugar, pulled-up grass, and apples. She hurled a handful at the horses, almost tripping over herself. The horses all darted back, frightened, but the stallion stood his ground. He threw back his head and sniffed the salty air.

"That's right, sniff it," Molly said quietly. "It's good. It'll taste good."

Molly knew she had to keep moving just another hundred yards or so, but she had to get around the horses.

The big black horse pawed the ground in front of him; his huge hoof looked like a blacksmith's anvil. *To get kicked with one of those would hurt,* Molly thought. That was the last thing she wanted to happen. Already dealing with the sprain, a kick or a bite would completely disable her and then she couldn't complete her mission.

Molly took out another handful of carrots and apples and threw them even farther. One carrot fell within five feet of the stallion's front hoof. He dipped his neck and head down, snuffling the treat.

Molly smiled and watched. "Go ahead," she said. "It's good. You'll love it. Doesn't anyone ever give you a treat? Poor little horsey. No treats?"

The horse pranced forward menacingly, and Molly staggered back. "Nice horse," she said, holding out her hand as if that would deflect a kick or a blow.

The horse eyed her suspiciously.

What is he thinking? Molly wondered. Reassuringly she offered: "I don't want to hurt you. I want to help you. I like you. I like all of you."

The horse stood quiet and still. She wasn't sure whether to speak or wait. Then the big stallion clopped forward to one of the carrots. He bent down and sniffed it, then raised his head, ducked, and whinnied. A second later, he gobbled up the carrot and chomped it in one magnificent bite.

"That's it!" Molly said, clapping her hands. "Here's more."

She threw more of the treats to the horses. "Try that apple there. That's real sweet. And if you're good, I'll give you sugar, too."

The black horse suddenly whipped up its head and neighed loudly. Molly fell backward, hitting her rear end with a whump. In a moment, though, she realized the horse was either thanking her or giving her praise for the treat.

When the horse's large red tongue slithered out and gobbled up another carrot, she clapped her hands.

"That's it! Now have some more."

The big horse stepped forward. All the others crowded around behind him. There were two foals in the group. They looked frightened, skittish, even more than the mares standing around the stallion. Molly wondered if the stallion drove out all the other males. Were they on another part of the island? There wasn't much time to wonder, because the horses nosed forward, grabbing the carrots, apples, and sugar cubes in their teeth and chewing eagerly.

Molly began throwing the food out to her left so that she could go around the horses. They followed the line of her throw and soon were eating to her left, out of the way.

Molly gave them everything in her pack then hobbled toward her destination. The stallion reared back at the last moment, churned the air with his front hooves, and whinnied.

She laughed. "You're welcome!"

The black horse turned to the others, and several of them whinnied, jostling their heads up and down as if laughing.

"Anytime," Molly said, waving. Then she turned and limped as quickly as she could toward the houses. Mr. Tomoro's was the closest. But Molly saw a figure standing on the porch of Mrs. Newton's home. She hesitated, then realized Mr. Tomoro might not be up, and precious minutes would be wasted.

"Help!" she cried. "Someone's trying to hurt the horses!"

The woman turned toward Molly. She was a skinny lady with sharp, angular features, a small nose, and a tired, unhappy mouth.

"Come here, child," the widow called to her. "What's the matter?"

"The horses!" Molly cried. "Some men are trying to shoot a disease into them with a hypodermic gun."

"Oh my!" the widow cried. "That's awful. Come in, and we'll call the police."

Molly staggered to the porch, taking the last few steps by hopping on her good leg. "They may have real guns, too, and they were trying to harm the horses. And they got my brother, Nick, and our friend John. They were mean to them."

"Come inside," the widow said, visibly upset. She opened the porch door. "Let me call the police right now."

Mrs. Newton held her hand out to Molly and smiled a rickety smile. Molly went past her into the house and looked around. There were lots of antiques and expensive-looking furniture. It was much nicer than their rental house.

Mrs. Newton's Doberman gave her a sniff then sank down to the floor.

"This is a nice place," Molly said.

"I like it," the lady said, leading her to a chair. "Sit down. You're hurt."

"Yeah, I twisted my ankle running so hard."

"You must be very brave."

"Not really. Please call the police. Please call now."

The Doberman watched Molly with slit, menacing eyes. She sensed him studying her. Something was wrong.

%℘ Eighteen

Nick and John
Begin Their Escape

From the crow's nest, Kelly had followed the horses with her video camera as they galloped within several hundred feet of the last house on the street. For a moment, they had stopped and congregated in an open area, snorting and jostling one another.

"I can't believe everyone's missing this," she cried.

A moment later, she spotted Molly on the far side of the horses. *What is she doing?* Kelly wondered. Then: *She's limping! But where are John and the others?* Kelly trained the video camera on the horses and began shooting as Molly threw the treats in her pack at the horses.

"This is great," Kelly said. "The greatest. They'll all go berserk when they see this," she grinned. "And I'll bet John hasn't gotten any of it!"

Then Kelly took a closer look with the binoculars. Molly had moved around the horses and was standing just beyond Mrs. Newton's house. Mrs. Newton had stepped out onto the lawn, and Molly appeared to be talking fast,

97

motioning toward the dunes and looking scared. When Kelly moved the binoculars back onto the horses, Molly had disappeared from her view. *Why would Molly go into the widow's house?* she wondered.

❧

"I've got it," Nick whispered to John while the thugs were outside. "Let's put our hands together and try to open the knife. We can try to cut away the tape. You cut mine; I'll do you. Hurry, before those guys come back."

After seconds—that seemed like precious minutes—of fumbling with the knife, the boys were able to thumb it open.

Nick could hear his heart thundering in his chest. *If Ally plans to do something,* he thought, *now is the time.* He knew she'd caused the flat. He grinned, realizing what a good idea that was. *But what about Molly?* he wondered. *Where are the police?*

With his fingers on the knife handle, Nick told John, "Just hold still."

"I am!" John whispered loudly.

"Don't get mad," Nick said, trying to calm down John—and himself. Nick needed to keep his groping fingers steady to find the cutting blade. Then he had it. "All right," he said, "hold tight while I pull." He could cut the tape where it was away from their skin, but Nick knew there was no way to get the cuffs off their wrists without the key. He figured the key must be on the ring that Pack had taken to start the RV. Those were the only keys Nick had seen. *But how to get to them?*

Nineteen

Where Are the Keys?

Ally watched as Pack and Lug stood at the tire. She could see them from under the RV, their legs still, now stooping, now standing; they weren't going anywhere. Seeing her chance, she stepped out of the underbrush and walked forthrightly toward the RV, trying to step softly to keep her Nikes from crunching on the hard dune sand. The door was open. When she reached the steps, Ally stopped and listened.

"I don't know how to use this jack!" Pack exclaimed.

"It's just a regular jack, man."

"Then you work it out."

Someone threw the jack onto the ground.

"I'll loosen the lug nuts. You figure out the jack!" Lug shouted. It was obvious neither of them knew what he was doing.

"Good," Ally whispered and slinked onto the first step. It creaked and Ally waited, relieving the pressure by relaxing her foot.

"What was that?" Lug said.

"How should I know?" Pack answered.

"I'm gonna check the RV."

99

He started around. Ally knew it was now or never.

She stepped up silently and, once inside, glanced around quickly. The only place to hide was under the table, even though it was crammed with junk. Crouching down, she began to move the boxes of junk, garbage, and clothing, wrinkling her nose in disgust at the smell. Moving one box out of the way, she crawled below the table, clutching her legs and pulling in a box as quietly as she could. A second later, she heard Lug's boots on the stairs.

❧

Molly listened as Mrs. Newton dialed the phone number, hitting three buttons: 9-1-1, that was it, wasn't it?

Mrs. Newton began to talk. "Yes, sir, this is Mrs. Newton of 664 Pine Woods Lane. Apparently there's something going on in the horse preserve right now, some men trying to hurt the Spanish Mustangs. They've abducted two children. Yes. Thank you. All right. I'll wait outside."

The woman smiled and walked back in. "Let me go and pick up my housecoat," she said. "The police will be here, but it'll be a few minutes. Do you want something to drink? Orange juice, Coke, grape juice?"

"Yes, orange juice, please." Then Molly reconsidered. "No, I'd better go home and tell my parents."

"Oh, no, please don't do that," said Mrs. Newton. "We'll need you to tell the police where to go. And anyway, it might be dangerous for you to go back outside."

"Oh, all right."

Molly didn't think staying was a good idea. Her parents had told her a thousand times never to go into a stranger's house. But as long as Mrs. Newton had called the police, there shouldn't be any reason for her to run home.

The Doberman continued sitting in front of her, staring at her like she was a hunk of beef. Mrs. Newton pulled open the refrigerator door. She was a slight woman, but her grip in helping Molly up the stairs had been strong. Molly had an uneasy feeling in her stomach. *If she's such a tough old lady, why is she being so friendly?*

Mrs. Newton produced a glass of orange juice, set it on the table next to Molly, then smiled and said, "Drink up. I'll be right back." She went upstairs.

Molly moved her feet back and forth, caressing and kneading her ankle. She drank a little of the juice and waited uncomfortably. The dog watched her with unblinking eyes. His stare made her think she should leave as soon as she could but still be polite about it, of course. *Now or never,* she thought.

Mrs. Newton came back in a blue-and-white housecoat. "I'm going to look out for the police. I'll be right back," she told Molly.

Why did Mrs. Newton go outside? Molly wondered. *And why didn't she take the dog?* Then Molly realized that for all her friendliness, the woman seemed nervous. Molly stood up to go.

The dog growled.

Molly froze.

"I'm just looking is all," she said.

Molly sidestepped to the window. The dog rose menacingly but didn't advance.

Out of the window, Molly saw Mrs. Newton get into her car. She sat inside doing something. *A phone. She has a car phone. She's calling someone,* Molly thought. She tried to make sense of this. Mrs. Newton was talking to someone. But why was she doing it out in the car?

Suddenly Molly knew. *Because she doesn't want me to hear.*

Molly regarded the big Doberman and edged toward the kitchen counter where the phone was. Some phones, she knew, had a redial button that would dial the last number called if you pressed it.

Molly peered at the phone, then at the dog. "I'm not doing anything," she said, as the dog suddenly barked and growled.

"Okay, I'm just picking up the phone." The dog was quiet.

Molly scrutinized the different buttons and read the letters under each one. One said REDIAL. That was it. She quietly took the phone off the hook and pressed the button.

The redial beeped.

She waited.

Nothing happened.

She hung up and hit the button again.

The same beeps rang in the phone again. There was a pause as if the phone was waiting for more numbers. Shouldn't the police answer? Molly felt uncomfortable being sneaky and all. But what had happened?

The phone resounded. "The number you have dialed is incomplete. Please . . ."

Molly hung up. Something was wrong. She knew she had to get out. She decided to make a run for it.

Molly edged toward the porch, but the dog stalked her. She jumped when she heard a voice behind her. "You won't get out that way, Missie."

She turned around. Mrs. Newton was walking directly toward her, grimacing and motioning to the dog.

The Doberman stepped toward Molly with cold hate in his eyes.

Before Molly could react, Mrs. Newton had her by the arm. Now Molly noticed how powerful Mrs. Newton looked, even in a house dress. She was strong, not one of those weak, grandmotherly types. With an iron grip, she dug her fingers into Molly's biceps.

Molly screamed.

"That will do you no good, young lady." She dragged Molly to the chair. "You'll just sit here and Roscoe will watch you," she said. "You'll be quiet as a mouse. Correct?"

Molly looked into the old lady's eyes with terror.

Mrs. Newton said with a glint in her eye, "You shouldn't have broken into my house, Missie. Now you're in big trouble."

"Broken in?"

"Roscoe!" The dog bounded over and stopped in front of Molly. He sat back on his haunches and glanced at Mrs. Newton, who said to him, "Don't let her move, boy!"

Mrs. Newton left again, but Molly was stuck. Now the police wouldn't come at all!

❦

Ally scrunched up tighter under the table as Lug's boots stalked by. The phone rang, and Ally labored to quiet her breathing as she heard Lug grab the phone from the table.

"Yeah? You're kidding! You're right we got a problem. A big one. . . . I don't know what to do. . . . All right. . . . We're changing a tire now. We think someone let the air out . . . Okay, we'll be waiting."

He slammed the phone down, saying, "Stupid old lady," then lurched back outside.

Immediately, Ally pushed out the box hiding her and crept to the bedroom door. Nick and John lay there still fumbling with the knife then turned around in terror.

"It's me!" Ally whispered.

"Thank God," Nick said. "You're all right. We thought they got you."

"Not yet."

"We need the keys," Nick said, holding up his cuffed hands. "They're on the key chain, maybe in the ignition. We have to get them if we want to get out of these hand-cuffs." He handed her the knife. "Nice job slashing their tires."

"I just let the air out of one," Ally corrected. "But I can slash this tape." She began to cut the tape binding the boys'

103

legs together. When she was through, Nick and John stretched. "I thought I was going to die in that position," John said.

The cuffs rattled on the metal railings under the bed. "Can you get the key?" Nick said. He pulled the cuffs—but not much distance. "We won't get far this way."

"Let me check." Just as Ally started to open the door she heard Lug outside say, "Go in and start it. Move it about two feet."

"Get down," Nick said. "Get under the bed."

The two boys laid back down. Ally said, "I can't fit under."

"Okay, get on the other side of the door, so if he opens it, he won't see you."

Ten seconds later, the RV jerked forward just a few feet then stopped.

With the engine idling, the front door slammed.

"What happened?" she said to Nick.

"I don't know," he answered.

"I think he left it running."

"He definitely left it running," John said.

"Fine distinctions," Nick said.

Ally almost laughed. "Then the keys are still there," she said.

She crawled around to the door, creeping on her hands and knees out to the front of the RV. The keys, as expected, were in the ignition. The engine was purring brightly underneath her. She looked at the keys to figure out which were for the handcuffs and how to get them off. They were on a ring, and she'd have to be careful not to turn off the engine in the process.

Ally got the two little silver keys she thought must be for the handcuffs and in thirty seconds had them off the ring.

Then with a sudden cough, the engine stalled. Ally froze. Had she accidently turned the ignition key?

She looked at it more closely. *No, the engine had simply stalled.*

Ally sat there listening. The two men had been clinking around in the back.

"Better check it, Pack," she heard Lug say.

"Ah, it just stalled."

"Check it out."

Ally scurried back under the table, her heart still pounding. Pack's boots scuffed on the stairs, and he went to the seat. He rolled down the window and called out, "Just stalled, that's all."

"Well, leave it off then."

Pack went back out, and Ally wriggled out from under the table. She hurried back to the room. When she opened the door, Nick said, "Have them?"

She nodded. "But only two. We have to hurry."

"Get me out of here," Nick said.

Ally tried the different keys on the handcuffs. The ring on Nick's left hand opened, releasing him from the rail. Then the one on John's hand opened. But neither of the keys worked in the middle set that linked John and Nick together.

"Let's go," Nick said. "We'll just have to run this way."

"But you won't be able to run fast, and you could get caught."

"What else can we do?" Nick whispered.

"Okay," Ally answered, "but stay low. If those guys see us, we could be in worse trouble than we are now."

Twenty

Molly Escapes

Molly stared at the Doberman.

"How can you do this? What kind of animal are you?" she asked. "Don't you know the horses are in trouble?"

A growl rumbled in the dog's throat.

Molly started to stand.

Immediately, Roscoe stood up and bared his teeth.

"Okay, okay. Don't get in an uproar about it!" Molly looked around the room. On the ocean side was a porch with a door down to the dunes. But if she did manage to get that far, there was no stopping the dog.

She glanced around and saw the stairs to the upper level. Maybe that was the way.

Suddenly, tears burned her eyes. She was so stupid. John had said it enough times. She was too young. She never thought ahead. How could she have gone into Mrs. Newton's house like that when her parents had warned her millions of times not to do such a thing?

For a moment, Molly sank down on the seat and sniffled. "God, I'm sorry . . ."

107

But then something welled up in her breast. What had Ally said about trust and not giving up? She couldn't give up! "Okay," she said. "God, I'm trusting you."

℀

Kelly studied the scene through the binoculars as Mrs. Newton jumped into her car and sped off. The radio was reporting that the robbers at the liquor store had given up their hostage and were surrendering. Kelly wondered if Mrs. Newton wanted to see what was happening. *But this early? And why isn't Molly coming out?* she wondered.

Kelly picked up the video and kept it trained on Mrs. Newton's car as it wound around the curving road back to the main road. Suddenly she made a decision. She was going down to that house to see what Molly was doing and to find out where all the others were. This adventure was no longer fun.

After climbing down the ladder and rigging, Kelly trotted through the house. She thought about waking her father to let him know where she was going. *But no,* she decided, *he might make me stay.* Creeping out the door and closing it quietly behind her, she checked her backpack one more time. She had the video camera, binoculars, and a spare jacket. Stepping into the brisk air, she ran down the street, passing Mr. Tomoro's. At Mrs. Newton's front door, Kelly banged loudly.

Roscoe went nuts, whipped around, and ran to the door, barking.

Molly recognized her chance.

She bolted for the stairs, limping on her sprained ankle.

The dog pounded after her.

"Molly! Molly! You in there?" Kelly screamed at the door.

Kelly heard the dog's barking move back, deep into the house. There was no way she was going to open the door with that monster inside.

Molly reached the top level then disappeared into a bedroom just as Roscoe sped directly at her, growling.

Molly slammed the door in his face then fumbled for the lock and latched it tight.

The dog hit the door at full speed.

The door held.

Molly sat down for a second, her heart pounding.

A second later, she heard Kelly yelling from outside, "Molly! Molly? Where are you?"

Molly made for the window and pushed it up.

"Here! Here!"

Kelly whizzed around the side of the house and looked up.

"What are you doing up there?"

"Help me down! My ankle's hurt. Mrs. Newton is the one trying to hurt the horses!"

Kelly looked around and shook her head. "There's no ladder."

Molly pushed the lightweight screen out of the window. Behind her the dog slammed into the door with a boom that shook the walls. Quickly she climbed through the window onto a small balcony, then closed the window behind her.

"Wait! Wait!" Kelly yelled. "There are some old sofa cushions here. I'll lay them down so you can jump onto them."

"Okay, hurry!" Molly shouted. On the other side of the bedroom door, Roscoe was growling, barking, and chewing at the floor.

Kelly pulled the pile into place.

At the edge of the balcony, Molly backed over the railing, hanging on and dangling her legs toward the ground.

"It's about six feet down," Kelly said as Molly hung out over the roof.

A moment later Molly dropped. A shot of pain tore through her leg. "Come on," she said, getting up bravely. "Get Mr. Tomoro! We have to call the police!"

Kelly ran ahead, and Molly hobbled after her. Soon they were at Mr. Tomoro's door, banging hard. A minute passed before the old man appeared in his pajamas. "Molly-san!" he said. "And Kelly-san. What . . . ?"

Molly didn't let him finish. "Mr. Tomoro, there are people trying to kill the horses. They want to inject them with a disease. Mrs. Newton hired them."

"Her daughter. Her son-in-law," Mr. Tomoro said, nodding.

"What?" the girls asked in unison.

"He own big construction company. Wants the nature preserve to develop real estate!"

"That's it!" Molly cried. "I have to go back and warn Nick, John, and Ally about Mrs. Newton."

"But you can hardly walk!" Kelly exclaimed.

Molly turned to Kelly. "Go home and get our parents."

"Yes, go!" Mr. Tomoro answered, tightening the tie on his robe.

❦

Nick pulled John from the bedroom while Ally led the way. Suddenly they heard Lug shout. "Hey, the boys aren't in the room!"

"Oh, we're in for it now!" Ally whispered.

Both men looked through the dirty windows. "There they are! And a girl's with them. Hey, you!"

Nick yelled, "Ally—can you drive this thing?"

"With a flat?"

"With anything!"

Ally looked ahead at the driver's seat. "Yeah!"

110

"Start it." Nick jerked John ahead. "Let's close that door. Where's the knife?"

"Here," John said.

While Ally jumped into the driver's seat and turned the ignition key, Nick and John crouched in the doorway. Nick fumbled with the lever that pulled the door shut.

"Go!" Nick yelled.

The engine turned over and over but didn't start.

"Go!" Ally shrieked. "Go!"

The door began swiveling to the right, shutting as Nick got a grip on it. Lug came around and grabbed the edge just before it closed. Nick and John pulled the door shut with all their might, smashing Lug's hand. Lug jerked back in pain, screaming and falling backward onto the sand.

Nick pulled the door shut all the way.

The engine kicked in as Ally rammed the gear into drive and floored the gas pedal. She shouted in triumph. The RV pitched forward, rolling off the jack. Fortunately, the tire didn't come off as it jolted and coughed forward, gradually gaining speed. Ally fought the steering wheel as it twitched and turned in her hands like a live snake. She looked for a way out of the clearing.

The access road was straight ahead, a good half mile. In the mirror, she saw Lug and Pack running from behind. Certainly they wouldn't be able to keep up—even with an RV going twenty on a flat tire! Ally knew, because the fastest human doing a one-hundred-yard dash can't even reach twenty-five miles per hour.

Ally bobbed up and down in the seat, yelling, "Yahoo! We're making it."

"But where are we going?" Nick yelled.

"Anywhere but here!" Ally answered.

The RV rocked and tilted. It felt like a ship in a storm.

Nick stepped back up the stairwell and looked around. A second later, he spotted a box of tools on the floor. He said, "Let's see if there are any metal cutters in here. We can cut this handcuff and be loose."

"Right," John said, closing the knife and handing it to Nick.

They opened the toolbox and rifled through it. The RV bucked and pitched. The tools jostled around, and the boys could barely keep their balance. There were wrenches, pliers, screwdrivers, a hammer, screws, nails, and bolts, but no metal cutter.

"Wait a second," John said. "Can't you cut wire with pliers?"

Nick looked at him. "I don't know."

Ally yelled, "Hold on! We're coming into a curve."

"Where are they?" Nick asked.

"Right behind us. Running like madmen," Ally shouted.

"Try the pliers," Nick said.

John pulled up the yellow-plastic gripped pliers and set the chain of the handcuffs in the slot at the back. He squeezed but made no headway.

"It's too thick," he said.

The RV swerved as Ally hit the curve. "The main road is probably up ahead," she cried. "What should I do?"

"Turn right," Nick said, knocking against the wall by the stairs with John sprawling onto the floor. "Come on," he said. "Hurry."

"I don't see it!" Ally yelled.

"Where does this road go?" John shouted.

"I don't know. I'm just trying to follow it," Ally answered. The RV jumped like a fish on a line, but it was weighted by the flat tire dragging along.

"Let me hit the grip with the hammer. That might cut us free," John said.

"Go ahead," Nick answered.

Even with the RV jolting like a crazed moose, John somehow smacked the steel hammer against the pliers

112

with one hand. Instantly, the handcuff chain snapped. In a second, Nick had it apart.

"They're still close behind us. I haven't been able to pick up speed. I keep shimmying all over the place."

"Let's ditch this thing!" Nick shouted to Ally. "Look for a place to stop, and let's run for it."

❦

Mr. Tomoro—still in his robe and wearing shoes with no socks—ran toward the access road to the nature preserve. Molly came limping behind him. A moment later, they spotted the RV coming toward them through the trees.

"It must be them," Molly cried. "We should hide!"

Mr. Tomoro yelled back, "Run into bushes anytime."

Twenty-one

The Crash

Ally felt wet all over, hot and scared. The RV was like nothing she'd ever driven before. The combination of the deep sand in the dunes, the loose flat tire, and the winding access road made for a wild ride. The two thugs kept running after them. She and the boys would never escape unless she did something quick.

The road was straight for the next sixty feet or so, then it forked. She floored the RV, and the tires shot out sand as they spun ahead. Nick and John held onto the rail as the RV bucked and pitched.

"Be careful!" Nick yelled above the din.

"What do you think I'm trying to do?" Ally scowled as she swung toward the fork and the curve. She knew she should go to the left, back out to the main road—it was the only way.

Ally mashed the accelerator one more time as she screwed the RV down into the curve. The tire came off as she spun. The RV started grinding to a stop. Ally looked in the mirror and saw the two thugs gaining on them, gesturing and shouting. At the same time, a car was speeding down the left fork toward her.

"Car!" Ally screamed.

The driver tried to avoid crashing, but there was no way to avoid it. She smacked right into the center front of the RV. Metal tore. The three kids screamed.

Then all was quiet.

❧

"A crack-up," Mr. Tomoro yelled as he and Molly hurried along the path. He put his arm around Molly's back, giving her some lift so her full weight didn't fall on the twisted ankle.

"Who is it?" Molly asked breathlessly, leaning on the old man's arm.

"I don't see them yet."

"Hurry. Maybe it's Nick and Ally and John."

Mr. Tomoro looked at her and grinned. "Like Ninja warriors."

Molly pushed herself all the harder, wincing at the pain in her ankle and resolving not to let it bother her. "If something happens to them," she said, "I don't know what I'll do."

❧

Kelly poured out Molly's story in tears and didn't get far before her parents, the Parkers, and the O'Connors were throwing on shoes and clothes to run out the front door. "Back to the crow's nest," she said to the emptied house. Kelly kept her backpack on and started to climb. "I'm going to show them all," she said when she reached the top.

❧

Nick pulled himself up from the stairwell at the front of the RV. His forehead was bleeding. He'd smacked the windshield. "John?" he asked.

"I'm all right," John said, pushing himself up. He had fallen under the table and crawled out.

"What about Ally?"

There was a moan, and Nick found her to the left of the driver's seat, draped under the steering wheel. "You okay?"

Ally looked up at him. "I rolled in here. Probably the best thing."

"We'd better get out," he said. He peered out the window, looking for the two men, but didn't see them. He helped Ally up, and they swiveled open the door. Nick stepped out first, took a look, then whispered, "Come on." He held out his hand for Ally. John followed.

They crept around the edge of the RV, looking for Lug and Pack, who were nowhere to be seen. Then they went to the wrecked car.

"It's Mrs. Newton's car!" Ally said with shock in her voice.

"Is she okay?" Nick asked, standing up and trying to look into her car. "Can she help us?"

The door was open. Mrs. Newton was gone.

"Where is everyone?" Nick whispered.

"Let's get into the woods," Ally said. "Something's going on."

"But what about my camera?" John asked. "The guys carried it back to the RV. I need to get that film."

"We'll have to get that later," Nick said.

John looked despondent for a moment then brightened. "But maybe my shots will get me the Pulitzer Prize!" John drew courage and darted back into the RV.

Ally heard voices from the woods. It was Mrs. Newton, talking to those thugs like she knew them: "What are we going to do?"

"Your car is wrecked and the RV too," Lug said. "But we have to get out of here."

"I have my Jeep at home," Mrs. Newton said. "But everything . . ."

"You got us into this," Lug interrupted.

Mrs. Newton's voice hardened. "What evidence do those stinking kids have against us?"

"Plenty," Lug said. "The RV. The hypodermics. The film in the camera."

"Get the hypos and the camera and dispose of them," said Mrs. Newton. "That's our only chance."

Lug led the other two out of the woods, keeping a look-out for the kids. Then he ordered: "Pack, go to the back and get the camera in the compartment. The injection equipment is inside the RV."

"Don't come back without it," Mrs. Newton whispered harshly.

Just then John appeared again at the door of the RV. "It's not here!" he shouted toward the trees where Ally and Nick were hiding. The two spun around.

"I told you, John, we can get it later," Nick whispered.

Ally watched in horror as Pack came from the rear of the RV.

"Get out—now!" she yelled in a raspy voice.

John lunged down the steps and ran for the bushes.

Lug and Mrs. Newton, in their own hiding place, didn't move. They were watching Pack pull out the Nikkormat from the compartment at the rear of the vehicle.

"They're getting the evidence," John said. "That's what I'd do. See, there's my camera. I'm sure the lenses are wrecked."

"Look," Ally said. "Pack got the rifle and drug equipment. You're right, John."

"We should follow them," John said. "I want my film back!"

118

"Yeah, but look," Nick added. Mrs. Newton was waving a gun in her hand then gave it to Lug.

"What can we do?" Nick asked.

"Hang in there, Nick," Ally said. "God's helped us so far."

Nick grinned. "You're never going to let me live that one down, are you?"

"No way!"

Ally studied the scene as she, Nick, and John crept deeper into the trees. "Hope Molly got the police," she said, looking down the right fork in the road back to the houses.

Twenty-two

Mustangs to the Rescue

Molly and Mr. Tomoro rounded the curve. Right in front of them was the smashed RV and Mrs. Newton's car. "Someone may be hurt," Molly yelled.

They were less than a hundred feet away when Lug stepped out of the trees and trained the gun on them. "Hold it," he said.

Mr. Tomoro stopped and grabbed Molly. She yelled, "You hurt my friends."

"Shut up and stand still," Lug said. Mrs. Newton and Pack appeared behind them.

At that moment, Ally, Nick, and John stepped out from the trees. Lug swiveled around. "I'll take all of them!" he yelled.

Mr. Tomoro shouted at Mrs. Newton, "Why you do this, Irene?"

"That's none of your business, old man." The woman's jaw was set.

"You're a murderer," Molly cried.

"I'm just taking care of my property."

"By trying to kill innocent horses!"

121

"They're pests! Absolute pests, like vermin, like big rats!"

Mr. Tomoro squeezed Molly's shoulder and said calmly, "Take gun away, Irene."

"Be quiet, old man," Mrs. Newton said. "We'll do the talking here."

Lug started forward, waving the cocked gun. Molly knew there was no outrunning a bullet.

Suddenly, hooves rumbled on the sand. The ground thundered beneath them.

Sixteen Mustangs, fury in their nostrils, streamed toward the small congregation of people. Pack dropped the camera and the injection equipment and began running. "I ain't gettin' kicked again!" he yelled.

Lug tore up the road toward the RV.

Mrs. Newton froze.

Nick, Ally, John, and Molly all yelled at the same time: "The Mustangs!"

Coming in from all sides, the horses overtook the crowd easily. The stallion barreled by, then swiveled between Mr. Tomoro and Mrs. Newton, nosing in Molly's direction. Everyone could hear Pack beating a path through the woods, but it didn't seem to matter. He wouldn't make it too far.

Now the horses didn't move or kick. For a second, everything was still. Then Ally, a few feet away from the stallion, sidled forward closer to the horse. "You came back!" she whispered soothingly. "You came back to save us all."

The stallion twitched but didn't move.

"It's carrots and goodies that he and the Mustangs want," Molly said, laughing and patting her backpack.

"They're beautiful," Ally whispered, locking eyes with the stallion and then a mare behind him.

"And smart," Molly added.

Lug stood helplessly looking for a way out, a way to run. But everywhere he looked he faced large pawing hooves.

122

That moment, the blare of a police siren ripped the air. Lug dropped his gun, saying, "I give up. Welcome, Lady, to the real world." Mrs. Newton wrinkled her nose and looked down at him with disgust.

Mr. Tomoro picked up Lug's gun and dropped out the clip then pulled back the slide and ejected the bullet. "That takes care of that," he said.

The horses seemed jittery from the sirens but didn't move. They shuffled about anxiously but stayed in the road beside the kids until the stallion suddenly whinnied and leaped around. He led his harem off, disappearing into the brush almost as mysteriously as they'd appeared. As the sound of their hooves faded away, Mrs. Newton and Lug were taken away in handcuffs to the car where Pack was already waiting in the backseat. The police had picked him up on the way.

All four of the kids hugged and cried. "I was so scared they would hurt you, Nick," Molly said. "And then I sprained my ankle, and Mrs. Newton trapped me in her house with that Doberman."

"I thought we were done for, Nick, really done for," John interrupted.

"If not for Ally," Nick said, "we might have been." He slid a bruised arm around Ally's tanned shoulders. "You're incredible, girl!"

Ally returned the hug then punched Nick on the shoulder. "It was all of us together," she said. "I can't wait to tell Kelly all about the excitement. If only she had seen this!"

The O'Connors, the Parkers, and the DeBarkses drove up then, all in one car, looking terrified and relieved at the same time to see the kids, the police, and everyone.

"The horses, Dad!" Ally cried. "They saved us."

"Are you really all right?" her mom asked.

"We're all perfect, well, except for some scratches!"

"And except for my sprained ankle," Molly grinned proudly.

"Thank God," Ally's mom said as tears sprang to her eyes. "I never would have let you go if I'd known it would be dangerous like this!"

"You kids," interrupted Nick's mom. "You promised you'd come home at the sight of those men!"

Molly pleaded, "I never would have thought Mrs. Newton would try to kill the horses, though. We had to do something before it was too late."

"Yeah," John added, "we caught them red-handed. The girls stampeded the herd. I took pictures for evidence. Nick made sure those thugs couldn't aim their injection needle on target."

"We all worked together. If we'd waited, the horses would have been gone."

Nick's dad interrupted: "But you should have gone for the police immediately, like we said. You put your lives in danger."

Nick shook his head. "Ally kept telling me to trust God. Once we got into trouble, we knew that was the only way out."

"You trusted God?" Mr. Parker said, looking surprised. "That's the only way. . . . Still, next time I'm going with you to spot horses, crabs, beetles, or whatever it is you've taken into your heads to see."

The police car radio crackled as one of the officers called in his report. Ally, Nick, John, and Molly each gave a version of their story. Before long, a reporter from the mainland arrived and interviewed the kids, promising to make it a headline for the newspaper.

☙

Back at the beach house, a reporter was waiting, wanting to get a picture of the whole group. Nick, with John nodding nearby, spoke about how brave Ally had been to let out the air in the tire and then rescue them from the room in the back of the RV.

Ally smiled. "Only doing what you'd do, Nick."

"Even John kept his humor going," Nick said.

Everyone gathered together for a photograph, when suddenly John's dad said, "Where's Kelly?"

"I have everything on video!" Kelly shouted down from the crow's nest ladder. "Molly and the horses! Mean ole Mrs. Newton. The car and RV crashing, the horses galloping up to save them! Everything! It's a whole movie almost."

"You're all safe, and that's what counts," Mr. DeBarks said.

"But I'll be the famous one!" Kelly triumphed.

Ally started for her room, and Nick followed her.

"What?" Ally said.

"Thanks," he answered.

"For what?"

"For reminding me."

"Of what?"

"Well, you know," Nick stammered, "to trust God, I mean."

Ally laughed. "Now that'll get my attention!" She walked into her room and closed the door behind her, peeking out with one eye and smiling at Nick.

Nick gazed after her and laughed, saying, "Does this mean you'll go out with me when we turn sixteen?"

Ally just smiled.

The Wild Horses of the Outer Banks

This herd of anywhere from fifteen to twenty-five horses is one of the only herds of wild horses left in the world. Over four hundred years ago, Spanish explorers left their horses behind in the United States, and these horses lived for many years on Assateague Island off the coast of Maryland. Some of the horses migrated to the Outer Banks and have been there ever since.

Most of the horses are black and brown, but sometimes they are lighter colors. They eat mostly the wild grasses that grow on the island. People should not try to pet or feed the horses because they have been known to kick and bite. However, most of the horses are friendly and can be seen frolicking in the surf and running on the dunes like little children on a sunny summer day.

The horses are protected by the state and have a sanctuary on Currituck Island. The Corolla Wild Horse Fund was set up in 1989 to protect the horses and receives donations for their welfare.

Mark Littleton, a former pastor and youth pastor, is a writer and a speaker at churches, retreats, conferences, and other Christian gatherings. He is happily married to Jeanette Gardner and has three children, Nicole, Alisha, and Gardner, also known as Gard-zilla the Destroyer because, at three years old, he is able to destroy whole cities when left unattended for more than thirty seconds. Mark and his family have a dog named Patches and a cat named Beauty, who is afraid of the dog. Mark collects lighthouses, original paintings of ships, and hundred dollar bills. He is willing to add any contributions you might wish to make to his collections, especially the hundred dollar bill collection.